PRAISE  E

MW00466372

SIDE TRIP TO KATHMANDU

"Marie Moore's vivid story combines the thrills of vicarious travel with a baffling mystery. It's the next best thing to seeing India in person. If you've traveled there, you will love this book even more."
—Annamaria Alfieri, author of *Strange Gods*, *Blood Tango* and *City of Silver,* and writing as Patricia King, *Never Work for a Jerk,* featured on the *Oprah Winfrey Show*.

"*Side Trip to Kathmandu* is the third book in the Sidney Marsh Murder Mystery series by Marie Moore, who has now clearly established herself as a master of the mystery/suspense genre. Simply stated, Marie Moore is an exceptionally gifted author who never fails to satisfy her readers and leave them eagerly looking toward her next novel."
—Midwest Book Review Bookwatch

"Author Marie Moore is a retired tour agent and guide. Her Sidney Marsh murder mysteries are (in Agatha Christie fashion) enchanting tales with strange clues that leave readers in the dark until the end. *Side Trip to Kathmandu* is a fast moving tale with intriguing characters and unexpected plot twists."
—Don Messerschmidt, Portland Book Review

"This action-packed adventure was worth the wait as Sidney and Jay travel to India.... Suspects were few, but the suspense was aplenty. The mystery kept me involved as it unfolded and I enjoyed the many curving paths it took to narrow the

apprehension to the killer.... A great read, a great adventure, great dialogue, and the great team of Sidney and Jay."
—Dru's Book Musings

GAME DRIVE

FINALIST for ForeWord Magazine's Book of the Year: mystery category.

"Visiting Africa through Marie's eyes was a delight and joy."
—Molly Weston, Editor of *InSinc,* The Journal of Sisters in Crime, and *Meritorious Mysteries*

"Marie Moore has scored another triumph with *Game Drive.* Excellent!! It will keep the reader glued from the first page to the surprising ending."
—Shelley Glodowski, MBR (Midwest Book Review) Bookwatch

"Moore's safari mystery proves that humans are more dangerous than wild animals! Compelling and well written."
—Sarah Wisseman, author of the Lisa Donahue Archaeological Mysteries

"With a vividly picturesque landscape as the backdrop and surrounded by a great supporting cast, this safari mystery adventure is an amazing ride."
—Dru's Book Musings

"Lively, suspense-driven and with adventure throughout, *Game Drive* is an exciting mystery that quickly had me trying to out-guess Sydney."
—Wendy Hines, Minding Spot Blog

SHORE EXCURSION

"An appealing heroine tangles with murder and romantic interludes gone wrong in a tartly funny take-off on tour travel, with more twists than a conga line. Readers will be enthralled."
—Carolyn Hart, author of the Death on Demand series

"Anyone who has been on a cruise ship will appreciate the behind-the-scenes look at what goes on in *Shore Excursion*, murders notwithstanding. Sidney Marsh is an engaging amateur sleuth and the mystery in which she finds herself is creatively devised and vividly drawn."
—Mysterious Reviews, June, 2012

"This cleverly written mystery with its elaborate attention to detail will catch your imagination within a few pages .... It is hard to believe that *Shore Excursion* is Marie Moore's first mystery."
—Regis Schilken, Blogcritics

"I really enjoyed this book .... The author gives a lot of handy tips for international travel. That aspect of the book was just as interesting as the mystery .... A lot of times, I have a fairly good idea of the motive behind the murder. But this one, not a clue."
—The Bluestocking Guide

"Graced with humor, a striking cast of characters, masterful deception and really good writing."
—Wendy Hines, Minding Spot

"This delightful little mystery will amuse most lovers of the cozy mystery genre and of Agatha Christie's stories .... I can easily recommend this to mystery lovers. It'd make a great beach read."
—Valentina Cano, Carrabosse's Library

"Moore's debut novel is a winner. Her world was so descriptive that I felt as though I was on the journey with the High Steppers. Also, the conclusion was satisfying; especially with the unexpected twist just when I thought the mystery was solved."
—Kellie, Simply Stacie

"A highly entertaining and fast-paced read."
—Lauri Meinhardt, Knits and Reads

"I love a good mystery and this debut mystery of Marie Moore's is just that .... A really good book and I give it a 5, so Marie you have a bestseller on your hand as I see it."
—Edna Tollison's Reviews

"Romance, adventure and quite a bit of mystery all tossed into one huge, compelling story."
—Yvonne, Socrates Book Reviews

"*Shore Excursion* is what would have happened if Nancy Drew had decided to become a travel agent. Sidney Marsh is stubborn and sassy."
—Chaundra Haun, Unabridged Bookshelf

"A crime novel that focuses on people and relationships rather than violence and gore. There's suspense, humour, romance and action. It entertained me and made me laugh while I also pondered 'who dunnit'."
—Dianne Ascroft, Author, Toronto, Canada.

"Brava Ms. Moore!.... A trip you wouldn't want to miss with a cast and crew you won't soon forget."
—Satisfaction for Insatiable Readers

Side Trip
to Kathmandu

Side Trip
to Kathmandu

A Sidney Marsh Murder Mystery

MARIE MOORE

CAMEL
PRESS
Seattle, WA

CAMEL PRESS

Camel Press
PO Box 70515
Seattle, WA 98127

For more information go to: www.camelpress.com
www.mariemooremysteries.com

Cover design by Sabrina Sun

Side Trip to Kathmandu
Copyright © 2015 by Marie Moore

ISBN: 978-1-60381-297-9 (Trade Paper)
ISBN: 978-1-60381-298-6 (eBook)

Library of Congress Control Number: 2014955980

Printed in the United States of America

ACKNOWLEDGMENTS

PATIENCE IS CERTAINLY A VIRTUE. Mohit would, I am sure, have some wise words to impart on its value. I can only say that I am most grateful to my hardworking agent Victoria Marini, to Catherine Treadgold and Jennifer McCord of Camel Press, and to Sidney's loyal fans for their understanding and patience in waiting so kindly for Sidney's next adventure to be written. Here it is, finally, and I hope all of you will think it worth the wait.

For Marie and Susanna, my precious girls, and little Kate, who I predict will grow up to be a great adventurer. Always, always for Rook, and especially for Doris, a brave lady who is a real team player.

"This is indeed India; the land of dreams and romance, of fabulous wealth and fabulous poverty, of splendor and rags, of palaces and hovels, of famine and pestilence ... the country of a thousand nations and a hundred tongues, of a thousand religions and two million gods ... the one land that all men desire to see, and having seen once, by even a glimpse, would not give that glimpse for the shows of all the rest of the globe combined."

—Mark Twain, *Following the Equator*, 1897

Also by the Author:

Shore Excursion

Game Drive

1

―∾―

"THIS IS YOUR FINAL CHANCE, Sidney," Silverstein said, slouching in his Italian leather chair and staring at me over his Cheaters. "And I really mean it this time. Your last two trips were disasters."

"Final chance, Sidney," echoed Andre, Silverstein's wormy little assistant.

I wanted to smack him. My chances were none of Andre's business.

"Mr. Silverstein," I pleaded, leaning forward in my chair toward the shiny expanse of his desk at the travel agency, hoping for some real understanding, "You must know that what happened on that safari was not my fault."

He tented his hands behind his curly gray head and leaned farther back in the chair, resting his head against his big, bronzed wrists. He studied me in silence, his stare unrelenting. He wore an expensive open collared shirt with sleeves precisely rolled to his elbows.

"Maybe not in the strictest sense, Sidney. Maybe not. But what about the trip *before* the safari … that nightmare of a cruise?"

"That wasn't my fault, either. I didn't invite a killer to come on the cruise. Surely you can't blame those murders on me?"

Sitting up, he extended his long arms, palms uplifted, into an elaborate shrug.

"All I know, Sidney, is that on the trips you've been leading lately, stuff happens. Bad stuff. People die. It may be just bad luck, it may not be your fault, but somehow it happens. And if your luck doesn't change—and I mean right now—you are out of a job. My lawyers are screaming. Itchy Feet Travel can't take any more unfortunate accidents. It's bad for business."

"Bad for business," Andre repeated, nodding.

"People are attracted to you, Sidney," Silverstein said, leaning back in his chair once again. "I'll give you that. They like you, they really do. You get high marks in all the customer satisfaction surveys. You are smart, good-looking and friendly, and in every other respect, you are a good agent. A class act. But your luck's gotta change, and that's the bottom line."

He stared silently at me for a beat, then he leaned forward toward the desk and his expression softened.

"You can do well on this, Sidney," he said, "if you stick to your business and don't go looking for trouble. Diana has the details of the assignment. Stop by her office when you leave here and pick up the rest of the paperwork."

Andre, hovering at his elbow, handed him a slim folder. Silverstein glanced through it briefly then passed it over to me.

"This should be a breeze, Sidney. I wish I was going. It's a great trip. You and Jay will be escorting a select group of high-end clients on a deluxe tour of India, followed by a side trip to Nepal. These people are the silver tunas, Sidney, a real catch for my agency. I can see a lot of fat commissions coming from this in the future, and we all know I could sure use some cash."

He wasn't finished. I started to reply, but he waved me into silence.

"Why, you may ask, am I giving you this plum? Well, I wouldn't risk sending you out with this group," he said, with a grim smile, "given your recent track record, but you have been specifically requested as tour escort by Mrs. Shyler. And as you know, we do all we can to keep her happy. She spends a ton with us. If Shyler hadn't demanded that you go with her group, you'd be on your way to Atlantic City with the gambling bus."

I breathed a sigh of relief.

Brooke to the rescue once again, bless her!

He rose from his chair, indicating that the interview was over. Clutching my new assignment, I grabbed my bag, followed Andre to the door, and was almost out of there when Silverstein's voice, calling my name, stopped me. I looked back from the doorway.

"Sidney," he said, "We're making big bucks on this. Don't screw it up. This is your last chance. And I really mean that. Understand?"

I nodded, pushed past Andre into the hall, and marched toward Diana's office to pick up the details of what might be my final job for Itchy Feet Travel.

♓

Diana was her usual snarky self, handing over the tour packet reluctantly. Her ice-blue eyes lasered into me. I stood in front of her desk, not willing to kiss the hem of her gown, but knowing that hearing her two cents was unavoidable.

"I really can't imagine why Mr. Silverstein is risking sending you out again, Sidney, especially with these special clients. I told him that he is making a big mistake."

"Thanks for the vote of confidence, Diana," I said, "I really appreciate it."

She patted a stray platinum blonde hair into place. It had somehow escaped her always perfect French twist. She smiled her wide, fake smile.

"I have nothing against you, Sidney. No matter what you think, I am very fond of you. But if it had been my decision, you would have been immediately terminated after the Africa trip. It's nothing personal. I am only thinking of the welfare of our clients. That is my first concern. Their welfare always comes before ours. Their happiness. Their feelings. Not mine. And certainly not yours. I am sympathetic toward the challenges you have faced on the last two trips. I have a very tender heart. But when it comes to choosing between your comfort level and that of our clients, your feelings just really don't matter."

What do you say to something like that? I looked at her in silence, struggling to control my emotions. Clearly, a reply was impossible, so I just stood there, waiting for the lecture to be over.

"As you know," she continued, finally relinquishing the envelope, "today is Jay's off day, so he has not yet been told about this trip. Normally, Mr. Silverstein would chat with Jay personally, as he did with you, but he is leaving tonight for LA on business. Mrs. Silverstein has a conflict and cannot make the flight, so I am accompanying him."

The sly triumph in her eyes was unmistakable.

"So we are allowing you to advise Jay of the assignment," she continued after she was sure that I'd gotten the message. "Please share all the information with Jay and tell him that I will speak with him about it when we return on Monday."

I perked up at that news. Telling Jay would be fun.

Diana smiled her phony smile again, showing all of her expensive, matching, gleaming white, perfectly capped fangs.

"I have every confidence that you will do a good job this time, Sidney. As you've been told, it's your last chance. I would actually be quite sad to lose you."

She waved her manicured fingers regally and dismissively toward me, swiveling around toward her computer and saying over her shoulder, "That's all for now. You may go."

As I closed the agency door behind me, heading down the crowded sidewalks toward the subway, I fully realized how sad *I* would be if I really lost my job. Given the recent state of the economy and the ongoing struggles of the travel industry, jobs like mine are scarce. Finding another one like it would be tough.

My name is Sidney Marsh, and I'm a travel agent, one of the last left standing in a job that everyone seems to think is becoming obsolete. Not me. I hope and believe that there will always be a place for a really good travel advisor, no matter what the Internet offers. I love planning trips for people and I pray they will always need my services. It's great making people happy. Plus, I get to go on amazing trips that I could never afford on my own. *Bonus.*

My career started about nine years ago when I came to New York for a summer internship with a travel agency, fell in love with the travel business and the City, and worked overtime until I managed to turn that little temp job into a career.

My mother, back home in Mississippi, nearly passed out over the idea of blowing off college and sorority rush for Manhattan, but she's finally gotten used to it. Sort of.

I'm happy about that, because I love my mom but I totally don't want to have to leave the energy of Manhattan and head back home for good if I can avoid it. Not right now, anyway.

My little hometown is warm and friendly, filled with nice people, good people, but it's tiny. I can count all the stoplights in my head if I try. It's a charming place, it's *home*, but it's not The Big Apple.

The agency I work for in New York is called Itchy Feet Travel. Our name sounds kind of goofy, but it appeals to people and we're pretty successful, even in these tough times. Like I said, some people think travel agents may be a dying breed, but in our shop we work really hard to send folks around the world happily and safely. We have good agents at Itchy, skilled, experienced agents. I'm pretty good myself, and Jay Wilson, my best friend and usual travel partner, is one of the best.

But the boss is right. Our last two big trips, a Scandinavian cruise and an African safari, unfortunately did not turn out well. Through no fault of my own, people really did end up dead.

2

~~~

I RANG JAY'S DOORBELL AFTER work with my elbow. My hands were loaded with takeout sacks filled with cartons of basmati rice, tandoori shrimp, chicken tikki masala, and veggies, plus a big jug of my home-brewed lemon and mint iced tea. Had to include the tea. I may live in Manhattan, but I was born in the South. In Mississippi, iced tea runs in our veins.

On my way to the subway, I sent Jay a text saying that I was coming over with dinner and a surprise. Our office is in SoHo, in Lower Manhattan, not too far by train from his place in Upper Chelsea on the border of Hell's Kitchen.

"They can't call it that anymore," he sniffs, referring to the label the neighborhood was given in the early nineteenth century. "There are so, so many talented, tasteful guys like me and my friends here now. We've raised the tone of this place, so now we're calling it Nell's Kitchen."

Jay's full name is Jeremiah Parker Wilson II. He was named for his stern and long-dead grandfather. Jay says Grandpa Wilson was an extremely quiet, dignified, and devout man, so it's probably a good thing he's no longer around to observe the fun-loving antics of his namesake. Grandpa wanted Jay to stay home in Pennsylvania, marry a sweet little wife, raise a bunch of kids, and run the family dry cleaning business. That wasn't happening. The minute they sang the last hymn over Grandpa, Jay was out of there, headed for New York.

Jay has been in this crazy travel business far longer than I have. His wardrobe is much nicer, and his apartment makes mine look like a hostel. He's clever, too; not much escapes either him or his wit. Tall and fit, at 6'2" and over 200 pounds, Jay's sheer bulk has gotten us out of some dicey situations. He claims to be my guardian angel. Guardian? On occasion, yes. Angel? Not so much.

Jay has warm brown eyes, wild red hair, and a Vandyke beard. The old ladies on our escorted tours adore him and I do too, although I'd climb the Chrysler Building before admitting it.

His spacious, high-ceilinged, rent-controlled apartment definitely raises the bar, even for his artistic street. It could easily be featured in *Architectural Digest*. Jay doesn't advertise it, but he did most of the work on it himself, including making draperies for the tall windows with close-out designer fabric and his grandmother's old Singer.

"Yum," he said, flinging the door open. "Indian? I could smell the curry through the door. Come in, come in, let me take that for you. You've bought way too much."

"I know. I always do. It was just so tempting."

"And iced tea, too," he said, unloading the cartons onto the counter and placing the tea jug on a shelf in his pristine refrigerator. "Good. Refreshing. You didn't get that at Taj Temptations."

"No, I left work early and went by my apartment first to brew the tea and change clothes."

He looked me over with his usual critical eye.

"That deep red color is good on you, Sidney, with your dark hair and eyes. You should wear it more often. Nice change from the black."

Like most of Manhattan, I usually dress all in black 24/7. The crimson shirt I wore was a birthday gift from one of my seven aunts.

"Thanks. Aunt Lucille sent it. Said it 'might help me catch a fella.' Hope never dies for my aunts and my mother."

"Well, you *are* getting on up there, old lady," he laughed. "What birthday was this last one, twenty-seven?" Jay is older than I am by at least ten years, but his age is strictly classified information. I can only guess how many birthdays he's had, because he'll never tell me.

"Yep. And still no ring on my finger. That worries them all a lot, especially my mother. I'm sure that her garden club has officially branded me an old maid."

He looked up from his task of gathering silverware and placemats for the table.

"How old was your mother when she married? You told me nineteen, right?"

"Yes."

"And the aunts, not much older, right?"

"All of them were married for better or worse by the time they were twenty-one, except Minnie. I think I told you; she's the one who never married. Mom's biggest fear is that I'll end up like her. No husband, and more importantly, no grandchildren. I get a lot of dire warnings."

Jay nodded and said with a grimace, "The Marsh Curse."

"Uh-huh." I sighed.

All seven of my aunts on my dad's side of the family have had bad, bad, *bad* experiences with men. They have been married, jilted, engaged, separated, divorced, in and out of relationships as long as I can remember. Men are attracted to these women like moths to the flame, but somehow it never quite works out. My mother fears that The Marsh Curse hovers over me as well. She may be right. My love life thus far has been anything but smooth.

Jay laughed as he lit candles.

"Might be true, babe, with your track record."

He poured me a glass of wine from an already-opened bottle and clinked my glass with his.

"Cheers," he said. "To Diana and Itchy Feet Travel."

"I'll drink to Itchy, Jay, just not to Diana."

"Agreed. Okay, take that evil witch out of the toast. To Itchy, then, and to me."

Now it was my turn to laugh.

He broke into his broad smile, then turned and began pulling down dishes from the top shelf for our meal. Reaching up into the tall cabinets for the bowls he wanted to use was easy for Jay. Even at 5'8", I would still have needed a stepstool.

After the lectures I'd been given at work, it felt comfortable and calming to be in Jay's beautiful apartment surrounded by candles and flowers and the aromas of the warming food. I felt the tension of the day draining away and finally began to relax. Jay's very presence was reassuring. I love Jay and he loves me. He is not just a coworker. He is my best friend.

"What about this surprise you promised, Sidney?" he asked, as he carefully placed the dinnerware on the counter. "Does it have anything to do with Athens? Have you finally accepted a proposal from Popeye the Sailor Man?"

"I'm saving my surprise until after our meal. You have to wait to find out. And it has nothing to do with Stephanos Vargos, thank you. Hurry up with all that, Jay. The president's not joining us. The table doesn't have to be perfect. I'm starving."

I busied myself filling glasses with ice and pouring tea as he finished warming the food and ladling it into bright, intricately painted and glazed serving bowls. Jay refuses to eat food out of cartons. The attractive dinnerware was from a set he had lugged home in the overhead from a trip to Morocco. I could never have managed that feat, but Jay is really strong because he works out religiously at the gym.

As I placed the glasses, silverware, and napkins on the handwoven linen table mats, I pictured my Greek cruise ship captain. Then I firmly forced my mind away from any thought of that handsome gentleman and any speculation as to where that relationship might be headed as I helped Jay bring the steaming, fragrant dishes to the table.

⟡

"That was excellent," Jay said, when his plate was empty. "Thank you. I'm glad you thought of it. I haven't had Indian in ages."

"Well, I'm glad you like it, because you'll be eating quite a lot of it soon. Guess what? The two of us are out on a deluxe trip to Delhi next Friday. That's the surprise."

"Are you kidding me? Really? Why? What group?" He thought a minute, "No. Not the High Steppers! Their trips are value savers."

The High Steppers are a group of senior citizens that Jay and I often escort on trips. Our last journey with them was a disastrous Scandinavian cruise.

"No, Jay, I don't think the High Steppers are quite ready for India."

He laughed, and draining the last of his tea, took his plate to the sink. "Maybe India is not ready for the High Steppers."

I smiled, picturing some of the quirky individuals in the group, as I followed him with my plate. Most of them would not enjoy India. High Steppers generally prefer more predictable excursions, with less spicy food and fewer surprises. India with the High Steppers would be one long complaint after another.

"Actually, from looking at the booking list, I think this new group is pretty much a mixed bag, Jay. I brought the info with me so you can take a look at it. It's small, only eight in all counting us, plus some assistants and the inbound Indian tour company reps." I rummaged in my bag, pulled the list out of his folder, and handed it all to him.

"See?" I said, as he began to scan the names, "Some are old, some young, some in-between. The only thing they really seem to have in common is that they are all extremely rich. This is a high-end trip."

"Even worse than High Steppers," he said, as he replaced the list in the folder and flipped it onto the glass top of his massive coffee table. "They'll be so spoiled. Nothing will suit them and we'll spend all our time trying to make things right. That's not good news, Sidney."

He poured himself a new glass of wine. "Another sip?"

I shook my head. "No thanks, I'm good. I think the trip will be fairly easy, Jay, because most, if not all, of these people are friends, or maybe friends of friends, of Brooke Shyler. She planned the tour. And she is why we get to go. Brooke demanded that Silverstein assign us to this trip. She said she would not book it without us, so he caved. Couldn't resist the cash, no matter how unhappy he might be with us. I'm unclear as to exactly what our responsibilities will be, though. Like I said, we're to be working in cooperation with an inbound Indian tour company."

"That's not unusual. We often associate a local company."

"True, but this time it seems as if the company may play a larger role than normal. It seems to be driving this bus, and at least one of their agents will be coming on tour with us."

Jay smiled. "Fine by me, babe. That can only mean less work for us! Let me take a closer look at this."

He set his glass down on the table and stretched his long legs out on the sofa, piling silk pillows behind his stylishly-cut red head. Then he opened the tour packet again and began thumbing through it. I curled up in a chair between the table and the window, enjoying the view of the trees along the row of brownstones. It was late August, and the leaves would soon be changing color.

Jay was smiling as he looked over the itinerary and the hotel list.

"Love the accommodations. Palaces. And Tiger Tops on the

extension! Real queens, the crowned kind, stay there. Did we book all this? This is a lot more deluxe than even the most high-end Silverstein tour."

"No. The Indian agency handled all the bookings. After Brooke called him, Silverstein worked out some sort of deal with them."

"Silverstein personally told you all this?" Jay asked, returning the packet to the table, "about the bookings and Brooke and everything? You had a conference with him today?"

I nodded. "And with Diana. Diana made me furious as usual. But Jay, they both said it was my last chance with the agency, and that if anything bad happens this time, I'm toast."

He shrugged. "If you're toast, I am too. We're in this together, Sidney. You go, I go. We're a package deal."

He reached for the bottle.

"Here, have some more wine. Pull that chair over closer, babe, and tell me all about it. Neither of us is working tomorrow so we've got all night. I want to hear it all. Everything that was said. Every word."

♓

It was after midnight by the time I'd discussed the whole thing in detail with Jay as we finished off the last of the bottle of wine. I was really tired when I climbed out of the cab and pushed the button for the elevator in my apartment building.

I had barely been able to scrape together the cab fare after my Indian cuisine splurge and had to shake change out of the bottom of my purse to come up with a tip. The driver clearly thought it was insufficient, pointing out that I could have used a credit card for the cab fare and the tip. He roared away in a huff.

The doorman, Jerome, is my buddy, and he yelled some Italian insult at the driver as he sped away. Cabs are not my usual mode of transportation—too expensive. I almost always take the train or the bus, but it was late and I was all in. Jerome wished me goodnight and told me to *fuggedaboutit!*

While waiting for the elevator, I grimaced at my reflection in the mirrors lining the walls of the deserted lobby. Not good. My long black hair needed more than a trim, and even the touch of mascara I wore had left smoky smudges under my big gray eyes. Jay says that with lashes as long as mine, I don't need mascara, and he may be right. Makeup habits are hard to break, though, especially Southern makeup habits. Like my mother and my grandmother before me, I'll never give up lipstick, no matter what. I feel naked without it.

The elevator shook and clanked its way up to the fourth floor before releasing me into the dim and dingy hallway. I practically tiptoed to my door, not wanting to disturb my neighbors.

As I unlocked the door and entered my dear little apartment, the fear of losing my job and having to leave the City that I love returned in full force. The heavy sense of dread I'd been carrying since the interview with Silverstein had become lighter in Jay's presence. In the late-night solitude and silence, it returned to overwhelm me. I dropped my purse on the table and switched on a lamp, looking around at my cozy little home.

My place is tiny, prewar, and nowhere near as stunning and grand as Jay's, but it is mine. I've worked hard to fix it up. I earned the money on my own to buy every stick of furniture I've lugged in from the resale shop, every picture on the walls, every lamp, plant and tchotchke, and I love it. Every last bit of it. I've scrubbed and polished, sanded and painted the entire apartment myself, with occasional assistance from Jay. The thought of leaving it and of leaving the energy that is New York City is too much for me.

In the cramped bedroom I switched off the lamp and curled up on my bed, still in my clothes. Then I totally lost it. I choked back the weeping only to answer the insistent ringing of my cellphone.

"Stop it." Jay's voice said.

"Stop what?"

"Sobbing. I know you are. I know you. Don't cry. Please don't cry, Sidney. I can't stand it when you cry. It will be all right, I promise."

"How do you know it will be all right?"

"I just know. That's all. Go to sleep. It'll be okay. Goodnight."

As the call ended, I got up off the bed, put on my pajamas, washed my face and brushed my teeth. I sat for a long time in the window seat, thinking, watching the lights of the city. Then I climbed in between the sheets and went to sleep, sound asleep, and slept until morning.

Like I've said before, Jay is my best friend, and he is always—well, usually—there when I need him.

3

<hr/>

SATURDAY IS LAUNDRY DAY FOR many people in my building, so most of the machines were already chugging away by the time I made it down to the basement with my basket, a little after 8:00 a.m.

I stuffed my clothes into the last empty machine, fed it some quarters, and pressed the start button. Nothing happened.

Piotr, our tall, wiry janitor, was busy mopping the gray concrete floor on the far end of the room, muttering under his breath in Polish. Someone had put too much detergent in a machine, causing it to stop up and overflow.

Being unfamiliar with Polish, I've always had a problem with Piotr's name. I used to think it was Pieter, but Janusz told me that's Dutch.

Seeing my dilemma, Piotr stood his mop in the bucket, smoothed down his gray-brown hair, and walked over to my machine. He gave it a solid kick with his sturdy black boot, and it immediately started filling with water. I thanked him and he smiled and bowed before returning to his mop.

It would only be a matter of time, I knew, before Janusz, our building super, appeared to call Piotr from that task to another, one likely far more unpleasant than mopping the basement floor. Piotr lives a dog's life, working dawn to dark under the lash of Janusz' tongue.

I waved at him as I left, and was rewarded with a brilliant smile.

Back in 4-C, I called Brooke to thank her for the India assignment, but only reached her assistant.

"Oh, hi, Sidney," Anna said. "Sorry, Brooke's not in town. She's at her villa in the south of France until the India trip. She said if you called to tell you she'll meet you in New Delhi."

"What about the rest of the group?"

"Everyone is meeting in New Delhi. At the hotel. They are coming in from all over and some are arriving by private jet. At least one of the group will already be there because she lives in India, in Mumbai. She's an actress. You know, Bollywood."

Oh. That explained why there was no air manifest in the packet, just e-tickets for me and Jay. I thought Diana had left the air list out by mistake.

"Well, when you speak with her again, Anna, will you please tell her that I called, and say how much I appreciate all this?"

"Sure will, Sidney. Have fun!"

"Thanks, Anna. I will. 'Bye now."

"Ciao."

After ending the call, I rechecked the packet and looked more closely at the printout of our e-tickets. The flight from New York to New Delhi was booked for Jay and me on Air India. Middle seats in coach. I didn't mind so much, but I knew long-legged Jay would be livid.

And he was.

The next day at the travel agency, he ranted and raged at our AirDesk, but nothing changed. No upgrade, they said. On specific orders from Diana.

"I feel your pain, Jay," Michael said, "but you know I can't change this reservation without her approval. It would be my job."

Jay stormed down to Diana's office, but she was not there.

She and Mr. Silverstein had decided to remain in California all week "on business." They would not return until after our departure.

His call to her cell went to voicemail. He sent her a text. No reply. He shot her an email, and an automated out-of-office reply bounced back to him.

"Sorry, Jay," said Roz, our receptionist, late that afternoon. She looked up at him from her computer screen. "I can't reach her either. Not on the phone, not on the computah. She and the boss must be … let's just say, occupied?" Roz grinned and fluttered her eyelashes so hard that I thought one of the big black lash strips might fly off. She liked Jay a lot and had stopped filing her nails long enough to try to help him track down Diana.

"Roz, do you know how long my legs will be folded up on that flight? Hours and hours. I'll be crippled. I'll be maimed. And I won't be able to sleep a wink."

He had really worked up a pity party.

"Yeah," Roz said, sticking another pen in her pouffed-up yellow hair and peeling the wrapper off of a fresh stick of gum, "I know, doll, the schedule says you leave Kennedy at three-ten p.m. and you get there the next day about the same time, three p.m. " 'Course, it's really not as long as it seems, because of the time zone thing. I'm not sure how to figure all that out. But it's a long time to be sittin' on your keister. That's for sure."

"Try her again, will you?" he begged. "Just try her again, Roz. That hateful hag won't take my call because she knows why I'm calling, but she might answer for you."

"Sure thing, sweetie, I'll keep trying until it's time for my train," Roz said, punching buttons again. "But I betcha she ain't answering no phones, Jay, and he ain't either. They're busy. You know what I mean?"

Without Diana's unlikely approval, odds were good that Big Jay and I were stuck for the long flight in the middle seats, nonstop, all the way to India. I didn't mind the cramped flight so much, but I did dread the long hours ahead of listening to him snivel about it.

"Give it up, Jay," I said. "We're in the back. That's settled, and you might as well make the best of it. After all, the land portion of the trip is deluxe. Try to focus on the great time we'll have once we get there. Remember, we could be headed to the Taj in Atlantic City instead of the Taj Mahal in Agra."

"Yeah," said Roz, "or going to the Jersey Shore next weekend with me. Who goes to the beach in September? We'll freeze our asses off, but Merv says that's when we gotta go 'cause it's cheaper. Go figure!"

She closed down her computer and picked up her purse. "Sorry, kiddos, I'm outta here. It's quittin' time and Diana ain't interested in anything we got to say. Have fun with them A-listers."

⊁

We actually got quite a lot of sleep on Air India after all, because the flight wasn't full. Whole rows were vacant in the rear section of the big plane.

Jay and I each claimed a row, pushed the armrests up, stretched out, and slept. Other fellow travelers were doing the same. It looked strange, but it was certainly comfortable. By the time we landed in New Delhi and emerged into the controlled chaos of Indira Gandhi International Airport, we were rested and ready to roll.

The first thing I noticed on emerging into the main terminal was the sound. Hundreds of voices, all clamoring in dozens of languages. Hindi is the official language, but India has fifteen officially recognized languages in addition to English, plus literally hundreds more, and even more dialects. It sounded as if all of them were being shouted at once.

The diversity was also evident in the faces, reflecting the

tremendous range of ethnicities that make up the population. India represents one of the oldest civilizations in the world, settled over time by Mongols, Greeks, Arabs, Turks, Persians, Chinese, Afghans and more recently by the Portuguese, French, Dutch, and British.

Outside customs a uniformed driver was waiting, holding a card high above the melee with our names printed on it.

I followed Jay as we pushed our way toward the driver through a milling crowd of peddlers, each eagerly hawking their wares or offering tours or taxi rides. The noise level was unreal, with everyone talking, shouting at once above a chorus of car horns. The blaze of heat from the late-afternoon sun and the rainbow of colors in the women's garments made it clear that we were half a world away from New York.

Jay kept a firm grip on both my hand and his bag as he muscled us through the bedlam toward the tall bearded and turbaned driver who had been sent to meet us.

"Come on, Sidney, just push your way through. We're almost there. You know what? Now that we're here, I think this trip is going to be the best yet. It's going to be great. I can feel it."

4

"**D**ARLINGS!"

Red hair and emeralds gleaming in the lights of dozens of candles, Brooke Shyler rushed to greet us with air kisses as we wandered, jet-lagged and starstruck, into her gathering of rich friends in the entrance hall of her hotel suite high above New Delhi. We hadn't wasted any time resting after arriving at the hotel. Neither of us wanted to miss a minute of the posh kickoff party for Brooke's tour.

Brooke wore an exquisite silver silk sari. As always, she looked perfect as she guided us into the suite's living room.

"Have some champagne—it's really quite good—and come meet my friends!"

As we followed in Brooke's wake, we snagged flutes of the fine vintage from a silver tray held by a smiling waiter. Jay's eyes were sparkling more than the wine. He was in his element, happy as he could be. I was happy too, despite being painfully conscious of how sad my little black number from the closeout rack must look in contrast to all the fabulous designer clothes worn by Brooke and her pals. We had checked into our rooms with just enough time to shower and freshen up before the dinner party, so at least my makeup was good and my long black hair was brushed and shining. Jay was splendid in his new dinner jacket. Heaven only knows what it had cost him. Jay would eat hot dogs for months if that's what it took to scrape up the money to buy a new outfit.

Brooke's select group of traveling friends was smaller than our usual tour groups. The eight of us included me, Brooke, and Jay, though also present in the long room were various personal assistants and hotel staff. Representatives from the inbound tour company who had made all the local travel arrangements were there as well, all humming around a short sweaty man who seemed to be their boss. At a nod from him, his minions began circling the small linen-draped tables set up for dinner, peering at place cards and leaving handsome embossed leather folders at a few places and imprinted tour folders at the rest.

"Cheap SOB is giving the good stuff to the big dogs and the budget version to everyone else," Jay whispered.

It was clearly an international gathering, with several languages being spoken. Jay speaks French and Italian and he plunged right in, but I could only stand beside him, watching and listening, sipping my wine, feeling really small-town Southern. The view from the huge silk-draped windows was of the magnificent sixteenth-century tomb of the Mughal Emperor Humayun, its massive marble dome illuminated and glowing in the gathering darkness.

Brooke raised her glass and invited us all to join her in a welcome toast. As she finished speaking, another tall, dark-bearded, turbaned Sikh leaned forward to whisper something in her ear. At first I thought he was the driver who had collected us at the airport. Then I realized that this man was taller than the driver. There was an air of authority about him as he stood behind Brooke with his arms folded, and it was clear that the dark eyes scanning the room missed nothing. His white linen suit was immaculate, but its formality did little to disguise what was obviously a heavily muscled and trim physique. Brooke nodded and clapped her hands.

"My dears," she said, "dinner is served. Please find your places. Then, starting in the far corner, table by table, we will follow Rahim into the dining room to be served from a buffet."

While we engaged in the pleasant confusion of finding our places at the small round tables, Brooke circled the room. She was working her special magic, putting me and everyone else at ease. The tables were perfect, overlaid with crisp white linen and centered with exotic flowers and floating candles.

"Lovely, isn't she?" the broad-shouldered man seated to my left said in a strong Scottish accent, as he watched Brooke moving from table to table. His sharp green eyes were rimmed with thick dark lashes and set under heavy eyebrows in a ruggedly handsome face.

His flight must have arrived just in time for the dinner, I thought, for his strong jaw was shadowed with a heavy beard. He had clearly not had time to shave or change clothes. His shirt was of good quality but rumpled, as was his jacket.

"She is indeed. Brooke is a wonderful person."

"Have ye known her long, then?" The green eyes focused on me.

"Four, no, almost five years. We both live in New York. I met her there."

"But you are not really from New York, are you, Miss Scarlett?" he said, in his deep burr. "You must be from the Deep South, judging from your accent."

Who are you to be talking about accents? I thought.

"I was born in Mississippi," I said. "And you are from …?"

"Fort William. In the western Highlands of Scotland, born in the shadow of Ben Nevis. My name is Adam MacLeod."

He picked up his leather folder and tucked it inside his coat as we rose for our turn at the buffet. Flashing me a grin, he said, "And I must call you something besides Miss Scarlett, my lady. What shall it be?"

"I am Sidney," I said, meeting the bold, green gaze full on, "Sidney Marsh."

The elderly turbaned man to my right spoke for the first time. His gray eyes peered at us through thick round glasses, as he said, "It is written, 'Among a man's many good possessions, a good command of speech has no equal.' " Then he nodded as if to himself and followed Rahim toward the dining room. I stared after the odd little man, wondering what on earth he could have meant. Such a strange and out-of-context statement!

With a bemused smile, I looked back to my left, but the Scotsman had disappeared, gone without another word. I saw him near the doorway, speaking with Brooke. Then I saw the door close behind him. Clearly, he wasn't staying for dinner. I was disappointed.

As I moved toward the entrance of the dining room, Brooke pulled me aside and murmured, "Sidney, I want a moment with you and Jay alone when this is over."

"Of course, Brooke, of course," I replied. "Brooke, we're both so happy to be here. Thank you for inviting us to lead this tour. We really appreciate it. And what a wonderful evening you've given us all tonight! Just let us know when you want to talk. Whenever."

Then she was gone, on to the next group, graciously greeting everyone with her merry laugh.

The meal, as expected, was delicious, as was the wine and the dessert that followed. Rahim kept a watchful eye on a parade of tall-hatted chefs as they offered us a fragrant variety of Mughlai dishes, served from silver bowls and platters. I chose a grilled and skewered lamb kebab and *Dum Pukht*, meat and chicken smothered in almonds and raisins and then braised in butter and yoghurt. A small helping of sweet saffron rice accompanied the entrees, along with aubergines (aka eggplant) cooked with ginger and lime.

A Hindu philosopher sat to my right and an Indian movie star who had arrived late was seated directly across from me.

In such company, the conversation was vastly different from anything in my experience.

"Hello," the actress said, in a soft, musical voice as the waiter helped her into her chair. "I am Jasmine, and you must be Sidney. Brooke has told me all about you."

She sat very still, like a beautiful statue, watching me. Her amber eyes, emphasized by heavy black liner, seemed to glow, and her skillfully applied foundation gave the impression that her skin was flawless. Pulled into a tight chignon, her gleaming black hair was accented by long golden earrings. Like Brooke, she wore an exquisite silk sari, though hers was in shades of crimson edged with gold. The chunky ruby and gold necklace around her neck surely cost more than my mother's Buick.

"Yes," I said, "I'm Sidney Marsh, Brooke's friend and travel agent from New York. It's a pleasure to meet you."

"And you are also from Mississippi, I hear," she laughed, "You see, I really do know all about you. But you must tell me more …."

It would have been a totally fantastic evening except for the chair on my left, which throughout the splendid meal remained vacant. While we were being served in the dining room, one of the waiters had discreetly removed the place service of the Scotsman.

I had a fascinating conversation with the Hindu philosopher, who also turned out to be an amateur fortuneteller hired by the Indian travel agency to go along with us on the tour. He was a slight man with thin hands and long fingers, which he kept folded quietly in his lap. He ate very little, only the vegetables, and drank only water. He wore a white turban; otherwise he was dressed in the simple white cotton clothing made famous by India's "Great Soul" or *Mahatma*, Mohandas Gandhi.

"My name is Mohit," he said. "It is my privilege to travel along with you and attempt to explain our traditions. I also have the ability to interpret any signs and portents that may occur."

Good to know. With my track record, I needed someone who could see trouble coming.

Music, coffee, and digestifs followed dinner in the adjoining apartment. We were seated in the central room of the finest suite in the finest hotel in Delhi. The central room was huge and the apartments connected to it seemed endless. Flowers and candles were everywhere. The sitar, the tabla—an intricate, long-necked stringed instrument—and its accompanying hand drums provided traditional background music at dinner. Afterward, the native musicians were replaced with a jazz trio.

I don't know if it was the food, the wine or the intoxicating experience of hobnobbing with the rich and famous in such an exotic setting, but it seemed as if the evening had just begun when Jay tugged at my elbow, dragging me away from the party.

"Time to go, Cinderella. It's beddy-bye for us. I'm sure you haven't noticed, but people are leaving. This party's over. Here's your key. I'll walk you to your room. Tell everyone goodnight and come along before you crash. I don't see Brooke. I think she may have already gone to bed."

"She told me she wanted to see us at the end of the evening, Jay."

"Well, I don't see her in the room and it's time to go. Everyone's leaving. Even that smarmy Indian tour guy and his peeps have gone. Brooke must have forgotten about us, or been called away. It's okay. We'll see her in the morning."

"I had a good time at dinner, Jay, didn't you? Really interesting people at my table."

"Yeah, I noticed. Well, I didn't. I wasn't so lucky. At my table, I couldn't get a word in edgewise for hearing this big blowhard from England go on about what a shame it is that India is not still under the rule of the Raj."

"You're kidding."

"I am *not* kidding. I thought the meal would never end. I was stuck there with him and this quiet little blonde named

Lucy, who is also English, but she lives most of the time in a villa next to Brooke's in St. Tropez. She spent the entire meal whispering and giggling in French with Justin, a filmmaker from Paris. He was seated next to her."

"What was his name?"

"The blowhard's? Felix. Felix something or other. Didn't get the last name. He was trying to imply that he is an earl, but I seriously doubt it."

I had caught a glimpse of Jay seated next to the burly red-faced Englishman earlier in the evening and knew from my friend's pained expression that he was not pleased with his dinner partner.

"That man seems a strange type to be one of Brooke's friends, don't you think, Jay? Not like her in the least."

"He's not a friend. He said he's her investment manager. He tried to give the impression that he's in total control of her finances, but I don't believe that either. I can't see Brooke letting that guy have full power over anything. I wish she hadn't asked him to come."

We picked up our folders—the cheap ones—and headed into the hallway.

Jay slowed his walk as we neared the elevator. He did not push the button to summon it, but instead turned to face me.

"Sid," he said. "Have you figured out why we are in India? Doesn't it seem strange to you that Brooke hired our agency and asked *us* to lead this trip when we're not really *leading* it? I was thinking about it during dinner while that guy was rattling on. I don't really see what we are doing here. We're apparently not leading much of anything. That Sharma guy and his people have done all the work. Why does Brooke need us?"

I saw in his eyes the same uneasiness that I'd felt during the introductions at dinner.

"It does seem strange to me, Jay. Really strange. I thought the same thing. Sharma is clearly in charge. He barely acknowledged us to the group, and he is personally accompanying the tour.

I can't see why we need to be here at all. But Brooke hired us, and knowing her, she has a good reason. Brooke may have all the money in the world but unless she's gone crackers she wouldn't just throw it away."

A slight movement in a narrow hallway on the left behind Jay caught my eye. Rahim was standing silently in the shadows, clearly within earshot, watching us. I wondered how long he had been there … and how much of our conversation he had overheard.

Seeing that he had my attention, he stepped forward, into the light of the foyer.

"Excuse me, sir, madam. Forgive me for interrupting. Could you come with me now, please? Mrs. Shyler would like a quick word with you both before you retire to your rooms."

Jay and I exchanged glances, and Jay shrugged and nodded. We followed the man down the dim passageway.

5

—✦—

"THERE ARE THREE REASONS WHY I wanted the two of you to come with me on this trip," Brooke said in response to our questions. She was smiling, but her lovely blue eyes, reflected in the mirror, were serious. She brushed aside her flaming red hair so she could undo the clasp of her necklace.

We were sipping coffee in the seating area of her suite's master bedroom, watching as she sat before the mirror at the dressing table, removing her emeralds and placing them in a velvet case. Rahim took the case from her, bowed, and left the room. Then she joined us, kicking off her Manolos and stretching out on the silk chaise lounge.

"In the first place," she said, with her brilliant smile, "you two are so much fun. You make me laugh! And you really are excellent tour leaders. Your presence will add a lot to my little excursion party.

"Secondly, it pleases me to thwart the intentions of those in your agency who would diminish or terminate you. For purely selfish reasons, I want you to remain in the employ of Itchy

Feet Travel for a long, long time. I like you both and I enjoy traveling with you."

Then she sat up and reached over to pour herself a cup of coffee from the silver pot. Her charming face grew serious, and she looked intently and directly at each of us. For once, she looked her age. Brooke has to be in her late seventies or early eighties, though she certainly doesn't look it.

There was no laughing tone in her voice when she said, "But the real reason that I want you along, my dears, is that I know I can trust you."

Brooke breathed a deep sigh, took a long sip of the coffee, and placed her delicate cup back in its saucer. She stood, walked to the window, and gazed out at the moonlit night. With her back to us, she said, in a low and deliberate voice, "I think one of my friends, one of my guests on this trip, may be a thief and possibly a murderer. I want you to find out which one. It shouldn't be too difficult, as there are only five to consider."

We " 'bout fell out dead" as my cousin Earline would say, on hearing Brooke's words. Jay looked as stunned as I'm sure I did, but then he recovered and laughed.

"You're kidding, aren't you, right? Good job, Brooke! You really had me going there for a minute!"

When she turned to face us, she was not laughing. Her face was sad, forlorn, and not a little angry.

"I can assure you it is no joke, Jay. I am deadly serious. There have been incidents that I will tell you all about. And accidents as well. Deeply disturbing accidents. I will only give you the basics now and explain further when you are better rested and we have more time."

Jay and I exchanged glances.

"Brooke," I said, "you know that as far as we can, we will always help you with anything you ask. But for something like this, shouldn't you be talking with the police?"

She shook her head. "I can prove nothing and have no clear suspect, so I have not gone to the police. But I felt that I must do something or forever regret my inaction when the worst happens. And something terrible *is* going to happen. I know it. I can feel it, feel the malevolence. It's here. I'm just not sure where it originates. Something is wrong. Someone is rotten. I know this. But with no proof, the police would only laugh at my fears and suspicions and think me just another crazy old rich lady."

"We know you're not nuts, Brooke," Jay said, with his easy smile, "and anyone who meets you would immediately see how sensible you are, even a stranger."

"Perhaps," she said, "but this conviction of mine seems so far-fetched that it will require much more than mere speculation to be believed."

I took a sip of my coffee but set it aside, for it had grown cold during Brooke's startling speech.

I looked up at her.

"Of course we believe you, Brooke. We trust your judgment," I said. "Tell us how we can help."

She smiled her sunny smile for the first time since our conference had begun.

"Sidney, I knew I could count on you. I have thought of this, night and day, for weeks, turning it over in my mind. And finally my thoughts began to gel into a plan. But to make my plan work, I knew I must have help. I needed someone I could trust implicitly, someone who would believe me, who would not think me paranoid or senile. I wanted someone with curiosity and a bit of experience in this kind of thing. An amateur detective. After several sleepless nights, I thought of you."

She sat in the chair beside me and gave my hand a pat.

I didn't comment. I was in shock.

"So what's the plan?" Jay asked.

"This trip," she said, "I decided to invite all the friends involved to come along as my guests on a luxurious excursion to an exotic destination—sort of a moving house party. It was my hope that the guilty one would not be able to resist the invitation."

"And make a slip, letting you know who they are," I said.

"Yes. And it worked. They have all come. They are all here, all five of them, in this hotel, on this trip, including the thief and murderer. And you two can help me catch them."

"Oh, boy," Jay said, standing and beginning to pace, "Here we go again!"

♓

"Why did you agree to help Brooke with this insane scheme, Nancy Drew? We need to be leaving on the first plane headed back to New York. You actually like playing detective, don't you, even though last time you tried something like this you almost got yourself killed!"

Jay had waited to vent until we were out of hearing distance of Brooke's suite and headed down the marble corridor toward our rooms.

"What choice did I have, Jay? Brooke's been good to me. She has never refused me when I needed her. Remember Africa? She saved my job. I can't walk away when she asks for my help."

"But this is a harebrained scheme, possibly a dangerous one. It's hard to believe a woman as sensible as Brooke could have cooked this idea up. She doesn't need us. If this is real, she needs a real detective, or the police. A pro, not Lucy and Ethel!"

He ranted all the way to my room. It was late and the hallways were fortunately deserted. We saw and heard no one else until we reached my door.

I fished my keycard out of my pocket and opened the door. Then I turned to look up at him.

"We're in, Jay. We're in unless you want to head back to New York and ask Diana for another assignment. Why don't you do that? Tell Diana you refused to help our agency's best client when she requested your assistance."

"I don't think our job description includes detective work, Sidney," he said. His brow was furrowed and his mouth set in a pout, a look that meant he wouldn't budge easily. "I know you love this stuff. I know you think you can solve this mystery, just because you've solved two others, no matter what the cost to us and our careers. You are just *aching* to solve this one too. I can see it in your eyes. But I also know that you are extremely lucky to even *be* here after your last little attempt at sleuthing. That curiosity of yours almost took you out, didn't it? And you were specifically warned, babe, by both Silverstein and Diana, to stay out of this kind of thing from now on, remember?"

Now I was pouting. "Well, I don't care about them. I care about Brooke, and if she asks for my help, she gets it. We won't be doing anything dangerous. All she asked us to do is watch and think and report back to her if we figure it out or see anything strange. That's not risky. We can do that. You can do what you want, Jay, but I've decided to help her. I don't think it will be dangerous for me to do that. And it's not dangerous for Brooke either. She will be safe. She has Rahim to protect her."

"And who's going to protect you, Sid? Who's going to protect you?"

"You are," I said, closing the door. "Goodnight."

⚥

Later, lying in the big bed in the darkened room with the pale Asian moon shining through the silk curtains, I did not feel so brave.

Jay was right, of course. The sensible thing to do was refuse Brooke's request, thank her for including us in her party, figure out a way to reimburse her for our expenses thus far, and return to New York. But I really didn't want to do that. Brooke had asked for my help and I wanted to help her. She has certainly been there for me in the past in a big way, and I am grateful for that.

Plus, bailing out would be awkward at best. Abandoning Brooke's plan could have a pretty bad economic effect on Itchy, which Silverstein wouldn't like either. Feeling that we had let her down, Brooke could angrily end her business with our agency. Although I've rarely seen it, I know a fiery temper comes with that gorgeous red hair.

And selfishly, I have to admit, I hated to give up this once-in-a-lifetime experience. I had never been to India before, and certainly would never again get to travel in such luxurious style. I was thrilled just thinking about seeing all that India had to offer, and especially looked forward to the following side trip to Nepal and mysterious Kathmandu.

I rolled over in the cool, silken sheets, plumped the downy pillows, and closed my eyes.

My last thought as I slid into sleep was that I was not going home, no matter what Jay decided to do. I was up for the challenge.

Not quitting.

Not bailing out on Brooke.

Not heading back to New York and Itchy.

Not going home.

No way.

6

"**W**ELL," I BEGAN, CUTTING INTO a slice of golden mango, "What's it going to be, Jay? Are you going or staying?"

He made a face and appeared to be giving my question some thought as he sipped his coffee.

We were seated near the window in the hotel restaurant, enjoying the morning sunshine and blue sky. Birds flew from branch to branch in the massive banyan tree just outside the window, and the light was bright, even at such an early hour. Though the sun was barely up, it looked as if the day would be a hot one.

"Staying, I guess. It's a long ride back, even though I gotta tell ya I'm not at all sure about this Pandora's box of a trip. But, after all, I guess someone's gotta look after you."

"Right," I smiled. "Good. Somehow I knew that would be the reason."

I tasted my omelet. As expected, it was delicious. I took a slice of crisp toast from the basket, passed the basket to Jay, and looked around the big room. No one else from our group seemed to be up and about yet. Jay and I were both early risers.

"If you're looking for the others, Sid, don't bother. I saw Adam MacLeod in the lobby first thing this morning and he said all the others were having breakfast in their rooms. All except Mohit, the seer, that is. He is seated cross-legged on the pool deck, facing the dawn. Some kind of meditation, I guess."

"Where is Adam MacLeod now?" I asked, trying to sound uninterested.

"Well, wouldn't you just like to know, Missy?" Jay laughed. "I saw you checking him out at the dinner last night, don't think I didn't."

"I was not."

"Yes, you were, and hanging on his every word. Bet you were super-disappointed when he bailed on you."

I *had* been attracted to MacLeod, and sorry when he left. If Jay had read me that easily, wouldn't MacLeod have done so as well? Now that was embarrassing.

I could feel the heat in my face.

"Now, now, pumpkin, stop blushing. Don't worry about it," Jay said, laughing harder and giving my hand a pat. "He likely isn't as tuned into you as I am. I've had lots of practice. If you really want to know, I'll tell you where he is. He's gone for a walk. Said he couldn't wait half the morning for the others to rouse."

"I wish I had gone for a walk," I sighed. "I always see a lot more when I am walking in a new place instead of whizzing by in a car."

"That's true. But given some of the violent crimes against women here that have been reported in the news recently, I don't think a solitary stroll would be too smart. You are obviously a young female tourist. Not a good idea to go rambling through deserted streets in a strange city by yourself. It would be all right, I guess, if you were escorted by a tall Scotsman. You'd be safe then—from the muggers, I mean."

His eyes were dancing as he spoke, and he would have delighted in saying more, I'm sure, but our Indian tour leader,

S.L. Sharma, had just bustled into the room and was fast approaching our table.

"Uh oh," Jay said. "Sharma alert. Here he comes. You know, I have no real basis for it, but there's just something about that guy I can't stand."

"What time are we supposed to meet the others?" I asked, rummaging in my bag, glad for even a visit from Sharma as a reason to distract Jay from his teasing. "I don't see my schedule. I must have left it in my room."

"Ten o'clock in the main lobby. If you need another schedule, I'm sure Mr. Sharma will be happy to give you one, though he's likely to add it to Brooke's bill. Finish your coffee. I don't want to linger over breakfast with this guy."

Sharma was wearing the same suit he had worn the night before, though with a different and even louder tie. The knot was as big as an apple. He wore a fresh lavender silk shirt with his belly straining the buttons and must have abundantly re-oiled his black hair. His strong cologne preceded him and made me glad I had already finished my meal.

"Please, may I join you?" he said. He pulled out the chair opposite Jay and sat without waiting for a reply. He carefully placed his bulging black leather briefcase on the empty chair.

"Good morning, Mr. Sharma," I said. "We were just talking about our plans for the morning. I seem to have misplaced my schedule. Ten o'clock in the lobby, is that right?"

"Yes. Ten o'clock. Ten sharp. We will go all together in a small coach for an orientation tour, pausing at India Gate for photographs. Then will stop at Red Fort for a guided visit. This afternoon there is free time for optional tours. And Mrs. Shyler has asked that cars be available for anyone who would like to go shopping."

He gave us both an insolent stare. His barely concealed hostility toward us was puzzling. I couldn't imagine how we might have offended him, since we had only met the night before. It didn't take long to discover his thoughts.

"You should have all the information in the tour leader packet you were given," he said. "It includes particular details that were not included in the packets of the special guests. I have been told by Mrs. Shyler to coordinate all the planned activities with you, though I believe that to be totally unnecessary. I do not understand it. Totally unnecessary." He shook his oily head. "There is no need for this," he said, his voice rising higher. "All the arrangements were made weeks ago, and the itinerary especially designed by me and my staff. I do not need or want your assistance."

Jay leaned forward into Sharma's space, towering over the chubby little man. "Look here, S.L.," he said in an even voice, "we know you didn't plan to work with us, and we didn't exactly ask you to dance either. But whether you like it or not, we are in this together. Because that's how Mrs. Shyler wants it. She pays the bills and she calls the shots. And things will go a lot smoother if you lose the attitude. We don't intend to disrupt your tour or alter your arrangements. We haven't run the numbers on what you are charging Mrs. Shyler for your services either. Not yet, anyway. And we likely won't, unless you make her, and us, unhappy. We all want her to be happy, right? But if she's not, if *we're* not, then it's a whole different ballgame. Understand?"

Sharma's face broke into a phony, toothy grin, but his little black eyes remained hard and glittering.

"Of course, of course," he said. "We must all work together in harmony. I desire nothing more, my friend."

He picked up the leather bag, opened it, and removed another tour packet, which he handed to me "with my compliments." Then, without another word, he rushed away from the table and out of the room, as fast as his chunky little legs could go.

"That was fun." Jay said, as we left the dining room and neared the elevator. "I'd really love to thump that little slime ball, Sidney. I know that between them, he and Silverstein are charging Brooke out the wazoo for this fancy little excursion.

And I wouldn't be at all surprised to find that there is an extra big piece of the pie just for old S.L."

"Did you see all the cash stuffed in that bag when he opened it?" I asked.

He punched the elevator button.

"Yep. But that's normal, nothing to get excited about. *Baksheesh.* Bribe money. Hard to do business in this part of the world without greasing the wheels. Sharma is an expert at that for sure. If I play my cards right, maybe he'll give some of that cash to me."

"Jay, you wouldn't!"

"No, babe," he said, laughing, "I wouldn't. But it was worth trotting the idea out there just to see the shocked look on your face. 'Bye. See you at ten sharp."

♓

The hard black eyes of the snake reminded me of Sharma's as it rose erect out of its basket to face the small brown man sitting cross-legged in the dust. The snake charmer was seated just out of the reptile's strike zone, though any distance would have been too close for me. I hate snakes.

A shiver ran down my spine as the scaly beast spread its hood and began to sway in time with the motion of the *pungi*, a bulbous, flute-like instrument made from a gourd and played by an orange-turbaned man.

We had just unloaded from our coach at the Chandni Chowk market stop, directly in front of the massive red sandstone bulk of Red Fort. Seeing us disembarking, the snake charmer had come running, his snake baskets swinging from a wooden pole across his thin shoulders, and hastily set up his gig. He was just out of sight of the fort's guards, for the Indian government has mounted an effort to stop the practice in response to pressure from animal rights groups. Laws had been enacted that were intended to protect the snakes.

"He is a member of the *Sapera* caste," Mohit murmured. "His father and grandfather were likely snake charmers before him. The *Sapera* are worshippers of Kāli, the Goddess of Time and Change, who is the consort of Lord Shiva. Her name conveys death. It is written, 'At the dissolution of things, it is Kāli who will devour all.' "

"I've had rather enough of this," said Lucy, who was standing next to Brooke. "Gives me the shivers!"

Lucy was a compact little woman with lovely blue eyes that crinkled when she laughed. I recalled how she had spent most of yesterday evening conversing with the Parisian filmmaker. Her precise British speech and erect posture spoke of her boarding school background. She was short, for her silver-blonde head only came to Brooke's shoulder as they stood together in the sunlight, watching the man and his snake.

"I agree," said Brooke, "let's walk to the fort and out of the sun. It's time to move on anyway. We seem to be attracting quite a bit of attention."

Peddlers and beggars surrounded our little group. We walked briskly toward the gated entrance, with Mohit in the lead and Rahim and Sharma shooing away the more persistent of the salesmen.

"Bloody pests!" said Felix, the big English money manager. "Filthy bugger! Get out of my way! Someone ought to arrest the lot of them."

His face, under the warming sun, was getting redder by the minute. In the sun's strong golden light I could see through the thin blond strands of hair to a scalp that was reddening too. Sweat beaded on his forehead and ran down the sides of his beefy face. His overheated condition was probably made worse by the number of drinks he'd consumed at the hotel bar after Brooke's dinner and the hair of the dog he'd had for breakfast. His hangover may have added to his bad temper as well. No one else seemed to be particularly bothered by the crowds or the temperature.

Red Fort loomed above us as we filed through the entrance gate. Once inside, the morning was suddenly calm, quiet, and pleasant again, for the teeming mass of peddlers and beggars are not allowed inside India's national monuments.

Red Fort, like many of the other forts and palaces, was first built by Shah Jahān in the fifteenth century. A World Heritage Site, it was the seat of power for the Mughal rulers of India for two hundred years. We entered at the Lahori Gate, which has emotional and symbolic meaning for the people of modern India. Every year on India Independence Day a flag is raised here and a speech given by the prime minister.

Just inside the outer wall we picked up a local guide, a pleasant, gray-haired man named Dave Patel. Dave led us though the first courtyard, explaining the history and traditions of life under the Mughal rulers, who were descendants of Genghis Khan.

I stood with Jay and watched our group gather in the shadow of the ancient Hall of Public Audience. With a pleasant breeze blowing and a bird singing from his perch on the dazzling marble pavilion before us, it was hard to concentrate on the complex history that Dave was rattling off in his sing-song voice. Numbed by his rapid-fire delivery of facts and figures, my mind wandered back to Brooke's startling revelations and suspicions.

I could hardly wrap my brain around the idea that one of my companions might actually be a thief and murderer. I looked at them, now lounging on the marble steps in the sunlight as they listened politely or pretended to listen to Dave spout facts. Yet it must be so. Brooke certainly believed that it was and was spending a lot of her treasure to prove it.

As Dave droned on at length about the military history of India, I mused over the puzzle, wondering how or if I could solve it. I knew that it would be difficult. All my fellow travelers were rich, smart, and sophisticated. Plus, the culprit must be very skillful to have eluded discovery thus far. It seemed an impossible task, especially since Brooke hadn't yet explained what had happened to make her suspect them.

I looked my new friends over as carefully as I could without appearing to stare. There was Adam, the interesting green-eyed Scot; Jasmine, the beautiful Indian movie star; Lucy, the tiny blonde expat Englishwoman; big Felix, also a Brit, who was unpleasant but hardly struck me as criminal; and Justin, the slim, clever Frenchman. Some were more attractive than others, but none seemed capable of the horrendous acts Brooke had described. Each appeared to be a normal, ordinary person just like Jay and me. Except, of course, that they were all extremely wealthy and we were definitely not. I intended to talk with Brooke further, as soon as I could, to learn more about her reasoning and the facts that led her to such a startling conviction.

"Please follow me now," Dave said finally, "as we enter the inner sanctum of the great Khan. The public was not allowed past these gates. This inner court was only for his personal pleasure and that of his courtiers, family and trusted advisors. Here we will see the Hall of Private Audience, once the location of the fabled Peacock Throne, the ruler's private mosque, and his harem."

Adam put his arm around Jasmine's shoulders and whispered something in her ear as we passed beneath the arch and through the gate. She threw her head back and laughed, smiling up at him with her amber eyes flashing and raven hair swirling in the breeze.

Jasmine was nationally known as a minor Bollywood film star. People stared at her in the streets because of her fame and beauty and sometimes called out her name. Born to a poor family in a small village in the Kerala region of India, she had moved to Mumbai and gained fame and fortune in the film industry. Or so Mohit had told me after dinner.

"He's invited her to join his harem," Jay whispered in my ear. "Bet you wish it was you instead."

I gave him a sharp look but didn't answer. He would hear from me later. Jay's favorite pastime is teasing me, and on this subject he was getting on my last nerve, as my cousin Earline would say.

7

⌇

THERE WERE FEW TAKERS ON Brooke's offer of private cars to the upscale Khan Market or a return to the Chandni Chowk after a lavish lunch of South Indian specialties. Only two cars were going from the hotel. All our fellow guests had visited New Delhi numerous times before and half of the group preferred to make other plans for the afternoon. Following the ten-boy curry lunch I suspected that those plans were only for a nap or a swim. Jay had informed me that the term "ten boy" means ten courses, each served by a different "boy" or waiter. In other words, a really large lunch.

Lucy, Felix, Brooke, Jay and I met in the lobby at 1:30. All chose the Chandni Chowk over the more modern Khan Market. Touristy as it is, browsing the Chandni Chowk is far more interesting than upscale shopping, and my fellow travelers already had all the luxury goods they could ever want. Jay loves designer things, of course, but only when they can be had at a bargain, so even he was content to skip the high-priced Khan Market in favor of the ancient bazaar.

Located in the heart of Old Delhi, across from Red Fort, the Chandni Chowk has crowded, twisting alleys that lead into the

Khari Baoli, the main spice market. Goods of every sort, from tawdry trinkets to treasure, are there to be haggled over. Brass, silver, silk, linens, jewelry, cooking pots, herbal medicines, live chickens, all are crammed into the tiny shops. Jay and I were confident that the colorful sights, sounds, and aromas would transport us far from our normal shopping experience. We could hardly wait to get there. Even back in New York we had been excited about the prospect of power shopping in the old city.

But first, we were given a long car ride and the lowdown on our fellow guests by Brooke.

As the drivers stood at attention by their gleaming cars at the hotel entrance, Brooke ushered Lucy and Felix into the first car and sent them off ahead of us after telling them, "There you go, my dears. Your driver will take you shopping and assist you with everything. Have a wonderful time, and remember, don't pay the first price you are asked! Bargaining is expected and all part of the game. I am taking Sidney and Jay with me for a little extra sightseeing drive through Connaught Place and down the Rajpath, perhaps also by the embassies. This is their first visit to India. I know that, having been here before, you'd be bored with all that. If we don't find each other in the bazaar, we'll meet you and the others later at the Imperial Hotel for high tea. Have fun!"

Even before entering the car, Felix was barking orders at the hapless driver. Lucy paid little attention to his bad humor. She was all smiles, chattering away as she settled in the car with her shopping bags.

As the car windows rolled up I saw her open a bright purple tin and offer him one of the delightful crisp ginger cookies that Justin had bought for all of us in the hotel gift shop. Felix grabbed a handful, stopped cussing out the driver, and looked as happy as he ever looked—in other words, only slightly calmer and less grumpy. They were good friends, which I found amazing because she was so nice and he, so disagreeable. *She just knows how to get along with him*, I thought. They'd known each other a long time, Brooke had explained.

"Good job, Brooke," Jay said, nodding approvingly, as they drove away. "I have to tell you that I'm not exactly nuts about your boy Felix. Lucy is great, but Felix really doesn't do it for me."

"Not many people like Felix, Jay," she replied smoothly. "I really don't either, I must confess, but he certainly manages my portfolio well. Asking him along on this trip, with his distressing dislike of people of other ethnicities, may have been a mistake, but as you will learn, I had my reasons."

"Well, he really is crabby today," I said. "He and Jasmine had a spat in the hall outside her room just before lunch. It's hard to imagine a beautiful woman like Jasmine having any type of relationship with a man as unattractive as Felix."

"Jasmine apparently has lots of relationships with all sorts of men. I think his money is the attraction," Jay said. "Not his looks or personality."

"Well, they must have made up," Brooke said, "for I saw her sharing lunch with him, all smiles. I think you could say that Jasmine is volatile. A real prima donna."

We waved as their car rolled away, then we climbed into the backseat of the next one with Brooke. Rahim took the front seat next to Nigel, the driver. Brooke had already given instructions to Nigel, and as we left the hotel grounds, he turned the car in the opposite direction from the path the first car had taken.

"Now," she said, settling in as we picked up speed and gliding smoothly toward India Gate and the Rajpath, "we can talk without anyone overhearing. Our driver has closed the glass between us and he has no interest whatsoever in what I have to say to you anyway. I wanted to give you some background on the other guests."

For the next twenty minutes Brooke told us the histories of our fellow travelers, her friends and suspects, interspersed with comments on the buildings and monuments we were passing.

Everything we were seeing had mostly been built by the British during their rule over India. The stately imperial government buildings and grand vistas of New Delhi made it easy to imagine the pomp and pageantry of the British rule, when India was described as "the jewel in the Crown." The former splendor of many of the buildings was diminished, however, by the fact that some of the structures were in disrepair and showed signs of long-time neglect.

Brooke's running commentary was the most unusual tour narrative I've ever heard—a light dusting of tour guide spiel sprinkled over layers of gossip steeped in a brew of horrifying revelations about our new companions.

According to Brooke, she selected each of our fellow guests primarily because he or she had endured the sudden death of someone close to them under questionable circumstances. Each one had inherited a great deal of money as a result. Suspicion, in some degree, had therefore been attached to each one following the tragic events. The facts on our new friends, winnowed from all the rumor and innuendo, were these:

1. Adam's young and beautiful wife had been the heiress to a manufacturing fortune. She had fallen into the sea and drowned while walking on a rocky cliff path on the coast of Cornwall in the first year of their marriage. There was some local chatter that she might have been pushed or the pathway stones loosened, but those theories were discounted as gossip by the authorities. Adam was her sole heir. He had never remarried but was often rumored to be in one relationship or another.

2. Lucy had been married twice and inherited a fortune from each husband. The first husband died of food poisoning on a business trip to China. Lucy was in England at the time and was reported to be devastated by the news. In her sorrow she was comforted, some said physically, by her long-time friend, Felix. After several years had passed, she married again, this husband wealthier than the first. The second husband was hit

by a car and killed coming home from a pub on a foggy night near their country estate in Northumberland. The teenage driver of the car was distraught and insisted to the policemen that he'd seen a second figure in the mist, but that was never proven and his story was discounted.

3. Felix's business partner apparently shot himself in his office after a great deal of money was reported missing from the firm. The loss of the money, however, was more than made up for by an enormous insurance policy he'd taken out before his death in which Felix was named as the sole beneficiary. The firm had purchased life insurance policies for each partner in the formative years of the business, so the suicide clause had expired and no longer applied. The insurance company and police investigated but cleared Felix of any involvement in his partner's demise.

4. Justin's elderly aunt was strangled in her home by an intruder. There was no sign of a break-in, so some said that she must have known her assailant, but she had a reputation for leaving her doors unlocked. An itinerant housepainter was arrested for the crime. He claimed to be innocent but was convicted and was now in prison. Justin was his aunt's sole heir. She had lived frugally in a small village in Provence, saving every spare franc. That savings, her insurance, and the escalation in value of her home and the surrounding real estate ultimately amounted to quite a pile of euros for Justin.

5. Jasmine's lover, a wealthy and internationally known Indian film director named A.J. Gupta, was found dead in his bed of a drug overdose. Heroin. His death was a surprise to everyone because he had never been known to use drugs. He left his entire fortune to Jasmine, much to the dismay of his wife and family.

"So there you have it," Brooke said, winding up her fascinating tale of sudden death and untimely inheritance. She leaned back in her middle seat as if the telling had exhausted her. Her eyes closed and Jay and I exchanged glances. He shrugged and turned to watch the buildings along the wide street, the embassies of various nations. I also looked out my window at the passing scene, noting the fading display of former colonial power as evidenced in some crumbling mansions, even while sorting through the stories I had just heard in my mind.

As soon as we had left the hotel and Brooke's narrative began, Jay and I had paid scant attention to our surroundings, so absorbed were we in her stories of our fellow travelers. Every so often Brooke interrupted herself to point out one landmark or another, and we looked up, startled, as if we'd forgotten where we were. With Brooke's speech apparently at an end, we began to take more notice of the sights we were passing, but my mind was spinning. There was no conversation. Each of us was lost in thought, mulling over the lurid histories of our companions. Even Jay remained silent, which was most unusual for him.

Nigel, our driver, left the broad straight avenues of New Delhi—built by the Brits in the early twentieth century—and the big car slowed as we entered the narrow, winding streets of Old Delhi, one of the oldest cities in the world.

Brooke had, apparently, fallen asleep. Not wanting to disturb her, Jay and I remained silent, occasionally pointing at something interesting that we were passing.

Jay clicked off some shots with his camera of a *sadhu*, or holy man, clad only in a white loincloth and standing with his begging bowl outside a Hindu temple. A slight breeze swirled strands of the man's long, matted gray hair around his ash-covered face.

Our car slowed and carefully entered a narrow lane, threading its way around one of the white cows that roam freely in the streets. Cows are venerated by the Hindu people and not slaughtered for meat. The Hindu god, Lord Krishna, is depicted as a cowherd, and the products of the cow, milk, butter, yogurt, *ghee* or clarified butter, and dung are important to the well-being of Indian families.

I always try to read up on a new destination before I go there, knowing that I will get a lot more out of the trip as a result. This time, even on such short notice, was no exception. I had stayed up late the night before leaving, reading and trying to get some sort of handle on what we would be seeing.

In my reading I had learned that roughly eighty percent of the population of India is Hindu, with over thirteen percent Muslim. The final seven percent are Christians, Sikhs, Buddhists and Jains. Over six million additional people profess other belief systems as well, including a vast number of tribal religions.

Now, in the streets, evidence of this religious diversity and ancient customs was everywhere. Temples and shrines to various gods were abundant. Saffron-robed priests mingled in the crowded alleys and trucks of all sizes bore the symbols of gods on their front grills, primarily the trident of Lord Shiva.

"Each one of our friends," Brooke said suddenly, "has greatly profited from violent death." She opened her eyes, apparently refreshed from her brief rest. "I am serious in saying that I'm convinced one of them may have been the murderer of their loved one ... I just don't know which one."

"Maybe so, Brooke, and I respect your reasoning and your judgment," said Jay, "but I don't get you going to all this trouble and expense just to figure out some cold cases that have stumped the cops. I know these are your friends, but why go to such extreme measures to figure it out yourself? This little mystery excursion is costing you thousands of dollars. Do you care that much? Why bring them all here? And why involve us?"

"Because, my dears," she said quietly, with a sad smile and a forlorn look in her blue eyes, "one of these select friends has also tried to kill me."

We were so shocked by that statement that it took a few moments to take it in. For a moment I couldn't really comprehend what she had just said, but I believed her. In all the time since I had first met her, I had never once known Brooke to exaggerate or exhibit paranoia.

"Oh, no, Brooke!" I said finally, totally shocked. "Not really? How and why?"

Brooke gazed for what seemed a long time out of the window of the car at the passing stream of people, animals, and vehicles before answering. The car slowed even more. We were arriving at the market. The driver pulled to the side of the road and stopped. The car, stationed in the shadow of a building, was immediately cooler, just from being out of the intense sun.

She leaned forward and tapped on the glass separating the driver from the passenger compartment.

He opened the glass, smiling, "Yes, madam?"

"We'll just wait here a few minutes, Nigel, before visiting the market."

"Of course, madam, very good,"

The glass slid shut. Rahim got out of the front seat and stood beside the fancy car, waving away would-be salesmen.

Brooke heaved a big sigh. She had our full attention.

"I had a large cocktail party followed by a small dinner for Valentine's Day," Brooke said, in a small voice, for once looking her age, "at my house in New York. Valentine's Day is one of my favorite holidays and I always have a party. My Valentine's party has become a tradition among my friends. There were many guests invited for drinks, but only the people who are with us on this trip remained for the dinner."

She stopped, again staring out the window, then continued, a faraway look in her eyes.

"As always, marking the place of each guest at the table were delightful little boxes of chocolates—tiny red satin boxes—tied up with silk ribbon. I order them from that fine candy shop on Lexington Avenue as favors. The dinner was a great success. Everyone had a good time and exclaimed over the chocolates, but they did not open them, not then. They all took them home at the end of the evening, as you do with favors. Now you both know that I love chocolate. All of my friends know I love chocolate, even though I try not to eat much of it because it's so fattening. After everyone had gone, just before going to bed, I opened mine, took a nibble from one piece, and before long became violently ill."

"Brooke!" I said, shocked.

"Yes. Fortunately, I was able to reach the phone and call the doorman, who called my doctor, Dr. Rosen. He actually lives in the building, so he came right away."

"Were you taken to the hospital?" Jay asked.

"No, at the time we thought it might have been the seafood appetizer—I don't always do well with that—or a virus. Neither of us suspected the chocolate. I was, as I said, quite ill, but Dr. Rosen treated me, stayed with me, until I was better. He felt that I would be all right by morning without going to the hospital and he was correct. But the next day, I thought about it and decided to have the remaining chocolates tested. Two of them were poisoned, including the one that I had nibbled. I am extremely lucky that it was only a nibble and not a bite. Had I eaten the whole piece I might not be here with you today. It was cleverly done. A tiny hole on the underside of each piece showed where it had been injected."

"What did the police say?" I asked.

"I didn't call the police," she replied, lifting her chin and defiantly squaring her shoulders, red hair flaming in the light from the car window. "I decided to handle it myself, and eventually I devised the plan for this trip. I didn't want policemen prying into my business and investigating."

"You didn't want the publicity either," Jay said.

"Exactly. The tabloid press would love it, wouldn't they? Just the thought of the headlines makes me shudder. I used a private lab to have the candy tested and the box examined, and paid enough to ensure that the result would remain private. The police were not involved."

"But Brooke," I protested, "this is so dangerous. As you said, if you had eaten the whole little box instead of a nibble—"

"I might have died. Yes. I am well aware of that, Sidney."

"Were any of the others sick?" Jay asked, frowning, exchanging glances with me.

"No. Only me."

She paused, remembering, then continued in a stronger, more determined voice, "I don't want any recommendations from either of you about calling the police. That's not why I told you this long story. It's too late anyway; I destroyed the evidence. I did keep the lab report, however. It is in my safe, just in case something does happen to me. This is why I arranged the trip, and why I wanted you two to come along. I know I can trust you. What I want from you two are your eyes and ears and good brains."

She smiled and patted each of us on the hands. "I want you to help me discover who did this. And when you have something to report, I want you to bring it directly to me, not the police. I hope I'm clear on that."

"Brooke," Jay said, "what about fingerprints? Wouldn't those have told the police who the culprit is?"

"I thought of that, and the box was examined when the candy was tested. There were no fingerprints other than my own."

"Gloves," I said.

"Yes." She squared her shoulders and picked up her purse, pulling out big round Chanel sunglasses. "There now. We've talked quite enough about this miserable business for one day. I say, no more conversation, no questions, no lectures. Come along, we're going shopping!"

And with that, she reached past me and opened the car door. We climbed out into the bedlam of the street and headed off at a rapid pace. She'd left us with no choice other than to follow her into the market, with about a million questions unanswered.

8

"You said this morning that your beard needed a trim, Jay. Why not give this guy a try?"

Jay shook his head and gave a thumbs-down on my suggestion as we watched a sidewalk barber lather a customer's face from a tin bowl held under the chin. He began to rapidly scrape the guy's cheeks with a long sharp straight razor, wiping the blade with each stroke on his apron.

"Pass," he said. "Don't want anyone with a knife like that near my throat. Come on, Sidney, enough of soaking up the atmosphere. We've got to hurry it up if I'm going to buy my turban and still have time to shop the spice market."

We had bargained our way through the bazaar, dodging weaving cycle rickshaws, motorbikes, chicken trucks and cow patties. Our distress over Brooke's dilemma and ours had eased somewhat when she left us on our own in the Pul-Ki-Mandi, the flower bazaar. She returned to the car, followed by Nigel, whose arms were laden with flowers. As she left she pointed us toward the Kinari Galli bazaar. She said that there we could haggle over saris and turbans. The car would return for us in an hour.

"Rahim will show you the way. Then he will leave you to wander on your own and return to the hotel to help me prepare for the evening. Nigel will return with the car and wait for you just on the other side of the spice market near the far end of the Chowk. He will take you from here to tea at the Imperial Hotel then back to our hotel."

"How will we find Nigel in all this?" I asked, waving my arm toward the crowded confusion of the market.

"Don't worry," she said, "he will find you. Just keep an eye out for Felix and Lucy. I think they're in here somewhere and perhaps by now some of the other lazy ones are too. They may have roused themselves enough to come on their own. Goodbye. See you at tea."

We waved goodbye and followed Rahim into the market. He led us at an easy pace past stalls selling everything imaginable, pausing whenever we wanted to stop for a closer look, helping us bargain.

Rounding a corner, he abruptly halted, grabbing my arm, to steer me around a large, steaming pile of cow dung.

"Look, madam," he said, "cow sits."

Behind me, I heard Jay snickering and repeating the phrase. I knew he was committing it to memory, storing up future cocktail conversation. He does that.

The sacred cows have the right-of-way. There are a lot of cows, so ... you get the idea.

When Rahim saw that we were comfortable with shopping in the Chowk, he pointed us toward the exit where, he said, Nigel would be waiting for us in an hour. Then, with one of his formal bows, he left us to return to Brooke and the hotel. We continued shopping our way through the market.

The lovely gold and silver embossed silken saris, in every color imaginable, were irresistible. I couldn't stop myself from buying a blue and silver one, even though I had no absolutely idea where I would wear it once we returned home.

The chances of Jay wearing the giant red turban he bought were much greater. In fact, he immediately clapped it on his head. Already taller by far than most of the people in the market, he looked like a crazy Western genie with the added height gained by the turban. It wasn't a real wound turban, but a tourist one. Little children stared at him as we passed and small dark women hastened to gather them out of his path.

The experience of the market was exotic, delightful, and only slightly spoiled by the distant glimpse we caught of Jasmine and Adam in a jewelry stall, shopping for earrings. She hung on his arm, laughing up at him. He carried several shopping bags stuffed full of purchases.

"Guess they decided this market isn't so touristy after all," Jay said. "They sure look like they're enjoying themselves."

He shot me a triumphant glance which I totally ignored.

Before we could catch up with them, however, they had moved on from the jewelry booth and were lost to sight in the maze of people, animals and merchandise. It was impossible to tell which way they had gone.

The spice market was fragrant with barrels, bags, and packets of every kind of spice, herb, and traditional medicine. Scents of cinnamon, curry, and cloves filled the air as sari-clad housewives bargained energetically with shopkeepers for small packets of the precious spices. We were nearing the end of it when we heard wailing and saw a commotion up ahead.

"Can't quite see what's going on up there, Sidney," Jay said, peering above the crowd. "I think there's a guy lying on the ground with everyone else gathered around him. We need to backtrack or find another route through. This one is blocked." He turned to head back the way we had come.

I was turning to follow him, but still looking back toward the commotion, when I suddenly glimpsed someone I recognized.

"Jay, stop!" I shouted, grabbing for his hand. "Come back, stop! I see Lucy in that crowd. Lucy's there! We have to see what's wrong."

We fought our way through the jostling onlookers and found not only a shaken, sobbing Lucy, but Felix as well, lying in the dirt. He was not conscious, and apparently not breathing either. His eyes were almost closed and his formerly ruddy face was ashen. A policeman was kneeling over him in the dust, attempting CPR.

Jay wrapped his arms around Lucy and shoved the looky-loos out of the way, shouting, "Move back, move back, give them some room, do you hear? Give them some air."

The crowd parted to allow the arrival of a team of EMTs with a stretcher. They began working on Felix, placing an oxygen mask on his face and strapping him to the stretcher. Then, with obvious effort, they picked it up and headed out as fast as their still, heavy burden would permit toward a waiting ambulance. I realized that the ambulance siren must have been wailing for some time. Up until that moment, with all the other noise and the shock of seeing Felix like that, it just hadn't registered.

Jay put his arms around Lucy and, following the EMTs, led her to the street in time to see the ambulance roll away, lights flashing. As soon as it was gone, the policeman took out his notebook and began questioning Lucy and the bystanders as to what had happened.

Distraught though she was, Lucy somehow managed to gather herself enough to give the officer a coherent account. Her low, soft voice seemed to calm the excited onlookers as they strained to catch her words.

"He had been complaining all day of the heat and was extremely red in the face, although he had stopped sweating," she said. "I knew he had a bad heart, so I convinced him to sit at this gentleman's table in the shade of his shop and take some tea. For a while he seemed better, but then he suddenly started shouting wild things and jumped up as if to run. That was when he grabbed his chest and collapsed."

"He called us filthy little yellow men," the owner of the stall added, "When this nice lady tried to hush him, he said she was yellow too. But then he said she was an angel with a halo."

It was clear that the owner of the tea shop felt little sympathy for Felix and a lot of sympathy for Lucy.

We were just thanking the kind shopkeeper for his assistance and turning to help Lucy to the car park when Nigel suddenly appeared, as promised, to lead us to the car.

There would be no high tea that day at the Imperial. We were heading straight back to our hotel to take Lucy to her room, and then we were going on to the hospital to find out what had happened to Felix.

"Thank goodness for you, Nigel," I said. "It's simply amazing to me how you could find us in this crowd. Simply amazing."

Nigel grinned and shook his head.

"Not amazing at all, madam," he said. "Easy." He pointed at Jay's red turban towering above the crowd, heading for the car.

♓

Much later that evening Jay paced back and forth in Brooke's suite until I thought he might wear a path in the carpet. Jay always paces when he's upset, and he was certainly distressed over Felix's sudden exit from this world. Rahim had greeted us at the hotel entrance with the bad news that Brooke's investment manager hadn't made it.

Jay ran his hands through his unruly red hair and said, "I mean, anyone could see that the guy was not exactly fit, but he looked basically okay to me. I think an autopsy should be done, don't you? I realize that Sharma is really in charge here, not us, but at the same time ...."

Brooke looked up at Jay and patted the sofa, motioning unsuccessfully for him to settle down and sit beside her. She had been shaken and saddened, of course, at the news, but she surprised me with her calm, matter-of-fact view of Felix's demise. While the rest of us were merely acquainted with Felix, Brooke and Lucy knew him best, had known him the longest prior to the trip. Most of the others had met him in New York through Brooke.

The evening plans for the group had all been cancelled. Instead Brooke invited me and Jay for a room service dinner in the dining area of her suite. Lucy had taken a sedative and gone to bed.

Brooke decreed that there be no mention of Felix's death until after dinner. Even so, the atmosphere was certainly not festive and the dinner conversation strained. Following the somber meal, we moved to the living room for coffee. I sat facing the window and the spectacular view of Humayun's Tomb, with its great dome gleaming in the moonlight.

"Felix had been living with a serious heart condition for many years, so this is really not unexpected," Brooke said, calmly stirring her coffee. "Everyone who knew him was well aware of his heart problems. Lucy was remarking on it just yesterday, and Jasmine sent her assistant to the pharmacy to pick up a prescription for him this morning.

"We were all concerned, but while Felix loved to give advice and orders to others, no one could give *him* advice about anything. He ignored the warnings of his doctors, refused the surgery that was offered to him, smoked, and ate and drank far too much. He said loudly and often that doctors were quacks and fools. I am saddened by his death. I shall miss him and his expert advice, but I am not surprised at all by what has happened."

"His temper didn't help, either, did it?" said Jay, with a grimace. "I heard him yelling at the maid after breakfast for disturbing his briefcase. Accused her of pilfering his papers. The poor woman was in tears."

"Felix was a hard man to like. While I admired his abilities, he was not pleasant and we were not exactly friends. But I shall miss him and certainly miss his guidance in my investments. He was superb with numbers. He really understood money and how to make it work. It is a shame that he could not have made himself more likable."

Jay persisted, "But don't you think an autopsy should be done?"

"Perhaps." Brooke shrugged. "I agree that an autopsy would give us a definitive cause of death, but if the doctors and the police think an autopsy unnecessary, we are hardly in a position to object. Things may change when his relatives are consulted or they may not. In any event, I don't see how a massive heart attack could be connected in any way to our other mystery."

"Brooke is right, Jay," I said. "It's sad, and I'm sorry about Felix, but I don't believe it has any bearing on Brooke's problem. His death, though sudden and shocking, can't be about Brooke. For once, I am grateful for S.L. Sharma. He has taken charge quickly and made all the required arrangements, thank goodness. He even called our agency and personally informed Silverstein. This is out of our hands."

"What about his family?" Jay asked. "Were they able to locate them?" Jay had stopped pacing and was calmer. He took a seat next to Brooke and reached for the coffeepot and a cup.

"Felix had no close family, Jay," Brooke answered. "He had three unsuccessful marriages, no children. He was the only child of elderly parents, both of whom died long ago. I think perhaps a cousin was listed as his next of kin. Mr. Sharma is still trying to reach someone."

"I think the only child thing may help to explain his personality," I said.

"Yes," Brooke said, "I agree. He was terribly spoiled. His mother doted on him, thought he could do no wrong."

"Well," Jay asked, "where do we go from here? Are you canceling the tour because of this, Brooke, or are we going forward? What do you think?"

"We will continue as planned," she said firmly. "Mr. Sharma is making all the arrangements, both for poor Felix and for us. Tomorrow morning at six a.m. sharp we will leave the hotel for the train to Agra. Agra and the Taj Mahal."

9

W OW. UNQUESTIONABLY A HUGE WOW.
The Taj Mahal, one of the world's most recognizable buildings, can only be fully appreciated when seen in person. And I was there. In person. Me, Sidney Lanier Marsh, all the way from Mississippi, standing smack in front of the Taj Mahal.

Wow. I mean wow.

As when you experience the power of Niagara Falls, no words, no photograph—no matter how skillfully or artfully done—can fully describe it or possibly do it justice. Its beauty is unspeakable, visceral, and compelling. The sight of the Taj drove all the sad thoughts of Felix right out of my head.

I stood just inside the massive red sandstone gate of the entrance, mesmerized by my first glimpse of this ancient monument to lost love. Even Jay, who is far worldlier than I, was stunned into silence at the sight.

We had arrived at the New Delhi station before dawn to board the train for Agra and the Taj Mahal, stepping gingerly around and over the slumbering figures of dozens of people. Whether they were waiting for trains or simply sleeping on the stone platform was unclear.

Our early departure was necessitated because of the light.

The seamless Makrana marble of which it was constructed causes the view of the Taj Mahal to change with the light. It appears rosy in the dawn, a stark, blinding white at noon, and golden pink in the sunset. In moonlight, it glows an ethereal white. To get the full effect, everyone who comes to the massive monument wants to view it all throughout the day as its aspect changes under the different lights. This is why multiple visits are common.

After a guided morning tour of the central structure, we would have free time to wander at will through the other buildings and gardens. Lunch at our hotel followed, and the afternoon featured a tour of Agra Fort. The following day we might even return to the Taj for a last look before leaving Agra for Varanasi.

The Taj was completed by a grieving Shah Jahān in 1659 as a monument and tomb for his beloved wife, Mumtaz, and its perfect symmetry amazes from a distance. Close up, the workmanship and beauty of the intricate designs of gold, silver, and precious and semiprecious stones embedded in its walls are staggering. It is impossible to stop staring. You simply cannot tear yourself away.

"Worth the trip, isn't it?"

I looked up from my trance to find Adam MacLeod's green eyes smiling down at me. The others apparently had gone on ahead. I could see the group following Rahim, snapping pictures, strolling alongside the marble reflecting pool toward the great dome.

"It's amazing," I babbled. "One of the most beautiful sights I've ever seen. The guidebook says it took twenty-two years and over twenty thousand workers to build it. Can you imagine? Isn't it wonderful? I can't believe I'm actually here to see it. But I was in such a daze, staring at it, that I'm about to be left behind. Now I'll have to hurry and catch up or I'll lose the group in all this crowd."

With a wry laugh at my idiotic yammering, he took my arm to prevent me from bolting down the path. I didn't know why this attractive man made me so nervous. I just knew that he did.

"Slow down, lass, there's no hurry. I told them I'd come back for you. Take your time. There's no rush. I'll see that you're reunited with the group. Easy now, easy."

Hearing his words, I *did* slow down, taking a deep breath and resolving not to act like a fool. I looked up at him as we walked together but he was not watching me. He seemed lost in his own thoughts. His handsome face looked sad, and in the sunlight, for the first time, I noticed glints of silver in his dark hair.

"It's beautiful, yes, but so sad," he said in his deep burr, staring at the dazzling marble as we neared the great dome. "She died bearing his child, you know. He never recovered from it. Losing the love of your life in such a way, so suddenly ... tears your heart in two."

I didn't comment, watching him carefully as we walked. I was thinking of the sudden death of his own wife, and I knew that he must be thinking of her as well. The lines in his tanned face deepened as he clenched his jaw. Had he loved her as this ancient king had loved his queen? Did he love her still? Brooke had said she'd heard mention of other women in Adam's life since the wife's accident, but none appeared to be lasting or serious.

Then his dark mood seemed to pass. He pointed to a grassy lawn on our left where a white ox pulled a mowing machine, guided by a turbaned workman.

"I'll wager you'll not have mowers like that in New York," he laughed.

I smiled, standing beside him as we watched the odd, old-fashioned contraption clip the bright green grass.

"Nothing here is like New York," I said. We resumed our stroll along the path beside the reflecting pool. "Except maybe some of the modern buildings. I've never seen anything like India before. Mohit says that India will change your life. I think he might be right."

"I agree. There's no other quite like this country. You'll not soon forget India."

"Have you been here before?"

"I have business interests in Mumbai, so I'm here quite often. Some of the others do as well. Justin is starting an export business in Goa that he wants Brooke to invest in, and poor Felix said he would look into it for her. He was also considering starring Jasmine in one of his films. I don't normally get this far north myself, and never have the time for sightseeing. But I must say I was pleased when Brooke invited me to come along on this trip. Even though I didn't really have the spare time, I'm quite fond of Brooke so I made it work."

The green gaze intensified and he took my hand in his as we climbed the marble steps of the monument. "I'm glad I did," he said, smiling back at me.

Woo-hoo! I thought. *So am I.*

But before I could think up a good answer, I heard someone shouting my name.

I turned away from Adam, dropping his hand, and saw Jay fast approaching. He had a big grin on his face that let me know I would hear more about Adam later.

"There you are," Jay yelled out before starting to fuss like an old hen, "I've been looking everywhere for you. Sharma wants to take a group photo, and I've asked him to take some individual ones too—in front of the monument—as we leave. Come along quickly, both of you, or there won't be time."

"Sorry," Adam said, shaking his head. "Afraid I don't do photos. I'll see you later, Sidney, Jay. Please tell Brooke not to wait for me. Tell her I'll get back to the hotel on my own."

And with that, he was gone, striding away into the crowd.

"Weird," Jay said, watching him, watching me. "Not exactly chummy, is he? I guess you could say he marches to his own drum or maybe bagpipe. I don't get him at all. But I can see why you hung back to be alone with him, holding hands and everything. He is definitely hot."

"I did not hang back to be alone with him," I sputtered. "I was taking photos and he just appeared."

Jay grinned, pleased at having successfully pushed my buttons. "*Whatever*. Now come along, Sidney, let's find Sharma's photographer. You know we need a good shot of us both at the Taj Mahal!"

Weaving through the crowd in Jay's wake, I looked back over my shoulder, but there was no sign of the tall Scot.

Jay was right, though. Adam *did* march to his own drum, and the man's abrupt appearances and disappearances *were* weird. So was his obvious aversion to photographs.

I wondered why.

This man was a puzzle, for sure. A puzzle I wanted to solve.

⊁

"Have a bite of this, dear," Lucy said to Jay, crinkling her blue eyes as she stood before him holding a fragrant, steaming dish of some unfamiliar vegetable concoction. She had picked the dish up from the buffet and was rounding the table, urging everyone to sample it. "It's quite delicious. Taste it. You'll love it. Go on, try it. Try just a bit."

"Okay, Mommy," he said, tasting the spoonful she had served onto his plate. He made a stricken face, then the grimace changed to a smile. "It's good. I like it. What is it? Give me some more."

"I told you so," Lucy replied serenely, giving him a large helping. "It's *palak paneer*, spinach with cottage cheese in a curry sauce. Sounds horrible, but it's really good. All these dishes are really marvelous, but you'll never know that unless you try them."

I tried it too. They were right. It was delicious. I thanked

Lucy and she smiled, "I'm glad you like it, Sidney." She moved on to another table, coaxing others to taste the dish.

"Why does she always do that?" Jay asked. "Every meal, she's like the star of some television cooking show, passing food, telling what's in it, how it's made. It's not as if you and I don't eat Indian food in New York. There are lots and lots of restaurants."

"Lucy says she hates it when people come to a different country and only eat what they eat at home. She's right, you know. If you don't fully experience the differences of another country you might as well stay home. And Indian food here is bound to taste different than what they serve in New York, where they've probably adapted it for American palates. She has a point."

"True, but it's a bit intrusive, this constant 'eat this, try that' thing she does. Every meal she comes around with something. You would think she'd cooked it herself."

"I think it's nice. I like Lucy."

"Did I say I didn't like her? I like her too. I just don't like having anyone push stuff on me."

"I bet you were a difficult child."

"I was not," Jay said, pouring more bottled water into his glass. "I was perfect. Ask around if you don't believe me. Mothers were always wishing their little boys could be just like me."

"Yeah, right," I laughed, trying to imagine Jay as a little red-headed boy. "I'll bet you were a terror."

I put my napkin on the table and stood to go to my room.

"Aren't you staying for dessert, Sidney?"

"Tempting, but my pants are getting too tight as it is."

"Yeah, I noticed," he said, in a sly, lazy voice. "Lucky you have a nice ass. I saw Sharma watching it when you went down the buffet line. Don't go yet. Stay a while longer. Why don't you just order coffee and talk to me while I eat my dessert. I'll tell you the latest dish on Diana. This morning I called Roz about that Machu Picchu trip we're booking for November, and I got an earful."

I ignored the tease and the bait and headed to my room, refusing to be tricked into keeping him company while he lingered over dessert and coffee. I've been around Jay enough to know how he operates. He hates to eat alone. And I didn't want to mess up a beautiful day with thoughts of Diana. I was more than happy to be half a world away from her barbs.

Lunch was basically over and the room was emptying quickly. None of our people were left in the dining room. Adam had not appeared at lunch at all, nor had Jasmine. I briefly wondered where they were, then dismissed my thoughts as adolescent.

At the elevator I was joined by Brooke and a solicitous Justin, who told me about a seer that Brooke had just engaged to read our palms during the cocktail hour.

"This man's name is Omar and he reads signs and portents even for people in the government," Justin said in his heavy French accent. "He is a dark and mysterious man, skilled at his craft, so he should be amusing, *oui*?"

"It will be fun," Brooke said, brushing back her cloud of red hair with long, emerald-clad fingers. "Different. He's arriving at five, after everyone returns from the afternoon excursion. Just come as you are, any time after that. I've ordered heavy hors d'oeuvres rather than dinner for tonight so we won't be rushed while hearing our futures."

The elevator was slow in coming. Justin bent to squint at the button through his thick but trendy black glasses. Realizing that the button had never been pushed, he gave it an impatient jab. Then he straightened and turned back toward us, again all smiles, smoothing his black hair down with his thin, white, perfectly manicured fingers. Justin wore his hair long, pulled back into a sleek ponytail. Tall and slim, he moved with the athletic grace of a dancer.

"You are missing the excursion, *ma chérie*? You don't wish to see this Agra Fort?" Justin asked Brooke.

"No, I'll be there," she replied, "but first I'm having a massage and a nap. I'm a bit tired from all the walking on this morning's adventure. It was a little too much for me. I haven't been feeling quite well. But one simply can't miss seeing all these sights, can one? A little rest and I'll be ready to go again. We won't be leaving for the tour until later this afternoon. I want to be refreshed for tonight too. I think the seer we've engaged will be excellent. I can't wait to hear my fortune!"

We had reached our floor. The elevator doors opened, and after saying goodbye to both of them, I turned left toward my room. Justin, ever the charming Frenchman, bowed to me then turned right to accompany Brooke to her door, saying that he would see me later on the tour.

As I walked down the hall, a door on the right opened and a waiter emerged from Jasmine's room, pushing a cart with wine bottles and the remains of a room service lunch. The meal had been set for two, and as the door closed, I heard a low male voice and peals of Jasmine's tinkling laughter.

So that's where they had lunch, I thought. *Adam and Jasmine. Better forget about that guy, dummy*, I told myself as I entered my room and closed the door quietly behind me.

Forget about him, girl. Don't waste another minute. He's not meant for you.

10

LATE THAT AFTERNOON, MOHIT LED the way with his wooden staff into Agra Fort, rushing us through the ever-present gauntlet of insistent salesmen and heart-wrenching beggars into the relative serenity of the courtyard. This visit was more hectic than our previous visits to tourist sites. Rahim had stayed behind at the hotel arranging the evening entertainment, leaving Mohit to be both guide and guard.

Even though he was physically small, Mohit accomplished both tasks easily, shouting admonishments to the crowd in Hindi and making grand gestures with his stick. I had no idea what his words meant, but they were effective, for the crowd fell back to let us pass.

Sharma had bustled off somewhere the moment we arrived at Agra Fort, saying that he would join us later.

Sharma had not asked for any assistance whatsoever from either me or Jay. We had expected to be given some sort of duties on the trip. After all, our agency was being fully paid for us to accompany the group. But so far, absolutely nothing had been asked of us by Sharma. We were treated as minor members of the group rather than tour leaders, and our input was clearly not welcome.

"This whole setup is so strange, isn't it?' Jay said in a low, exasperated voice as we followed the others through the entrance. "I mean, what's the point in us even being here?"

Justin had just asked Jay a simple housekeeping question for which Jay had no answer. On any normal tour we would have known such facts; however, Sharma had not seen fit to share any information with us.

"I don't know," I replied, taking his arm to slow him down as the group filed past us through the gate. I didn't want any of the others in earshot because I could see that Jay was about to blow. He was running his fingers through his red hair the way he does when he's upset.

"Well, it's embarrassing to be introduced as a tour leader and then be totally clueless," he said fiercely. "I hate it. I mean, I'm enjoying the trip, but it is all so awkward just because Sharma hasn't seen fit to share with us. Now Justin surely thinks I'm the biggest dumbass on the planet. Am I a tour leader or not? He doesn't know. I don't know. You don't know. I feel so stupid. I can't stand being made to look like an idiot when I'm a qualified professional. It stinks. This is the strangest gig we've ever worked."

"Yes, it is," I agreed quietly, trying to soothe the volcano that was clearly on the verge of erupting, "But Jay, Brooke says she only wants our eyes and ears, not our travel skills, so I guess it's okay. She's paying the bills so she calls the shots. And Silverstein said our main job is just to keep her happy. Still, I'm sure he must have expected us to do far more than we're doing. Do you think we should give him a call to touch base?"

He shook his now-wild red head.

"No. Bad idea, Sidney. No phone call. We wouldn't get him. He's off on a trip himself, remember? We'd only get Diana. Do we want to hear her advice?"

"No …."

"Well, then, a phone call is out. I'll shoot Silverstein an email tonight, fill him in, and ask him to clarify what he wants us to do. But in the meantime, before I hear back from him, I think I'll just have a private chat with Mr. Sharma."

He smiled a strange little smile, an intense look in his eyes.

"Jay," I said, recognizing that look, "you aren't going to get rough with him, are you?"

"If you mean, am I going to thump him, the answer is no. At least I don't plan to. But after our talk, Mr. Sharma will definitely understand that I won't be made to look stupid again, that's for sure."

And with that, he shook my hand off and marched on to join the group, leaving me to resolve not to be anywhere near when Jay had his "chat" with Sharma.

I followed him through the gate, joining the others just as Mohit began his introductory speech.

"Agra Fort, this most beautiful and strong fortress, was first built by Akbar, the great Shah Jahān's grandfather, in the middle 1500s," Mohit said, gesturing toward the massive walls with his stick. "This strong sandstone fortress defended the Mughal dynasty for the succeeding generations, who added to it, building magnificent pavilions, audience halls, and private quarters within. It was also where Shah Jahān died after being imprisoned here under house arrest for the last eight years of his life. His jailer was his own son, who had overthrown Jahān and taken control of the kingdom. I will show you where Shah Jahān lived while he was imprisoned in this most beautiful of jailhouses. Follow me."

Mohit told us the end of Jahān's story from the windows of the ruler's own personal apartment. Shah Jahān's beloved Taj Mahal, directly across the river, was framed by the window opening.

"Because of his son's treachery, Shah Jahān could no longer personally visit his finest creation, the Taj Mahal. He could only view it from afar, from this very window, until it was time for him to join his dear Mumtaz forever. It was an exquisite torture. And as you saw only this morning, he lies there with her now."

Everyone moved toward the window opening to fully experience the view that had been the deposed king's.

"What a wretch that son must have been!" Brooke said, gazing out the window opening with a faraway look in her eyes. "Betrayal by someone so close to you, someone you love, someone you trust. How bitter that is!"

Jay and I exchanged glances, knowing that she was not likely just speaking of the ancient Indian ruler.

Jay moved closer to her, and putting his big arm around her shoulders, bent to whisper something in her ear. Her sudden peal of laughter let me know that his words had been, as usual, outrageous.

There was no comment from the others, most of whom seemed unmoved by Mohit's sad story and Brooke's reaction to it.

Near the doorway stood Justin and Lucy with their heads together. They were murmuring in French and obviously impatient to leave. Jasmine was smiling up at Adam as usual, chattering away, twirling a strand of her shiny blue-black hair around a jeweled finger. For once, Adam paid little attention to her. He alone seemed lost in thought, staring over Brooke's head at the view of the Taj across the river, now glowing pink in the setting sun.

A sudden movement from the doorway caught my eye and I looked back just in time to see Sharma hand Justin a wad of paper, which he immediately crammed into his pocket without looking at it. Was it money? The movement was so quick I couldn't tell.

Justin glanced instead at Lucy, as if to see if she had noticed the exchange. She hadn't, for she had stepped forward to chat with Brooke and Jay.

Mohit had noticed, though, and seeing that I had as well, he gave me a slight smile and a shrug.

Sharma pushed back his coat sleeve to peer impatiently at the big faux Rolex strapped on his chubby wrist. "Ladies and gentlemen, we must go," he said. "The sun is setting. Follow me, please, to the cars, which are waiting out front. It is time to return to the hotel. Cocktails will be served in the garden."

I turned to follow, and as I went down the steps, Mohit quietly appeared at my elbow, saying, "Curiosity killed the cat, my lady. You have very big eyes. Perhaps it is better sometimes not to be so observant."

Startled, I opened my mouth to reply, but he was gone. I saw him moving swiftly ahead to the front of the group, pushing past Sharma, waving the big stick to ward off interlopers.

11

⚬

I'VE NEVER PUT ANY FAITH in good luck charms and
fortunetellers, but the turbaned seer Brooke and Justin had
hired for the evening certainly lived up to his billing.

Between the wine and the fortune-telling, there was a lot of
laughing under the Indian moon. Everyone loved having their
palms read, though my prophecy was a bit disturbing.

"I say, this is all rather fun, isn't it?" Lucy said, emerging
from the candlelit curtained alcove where the mystical swami
was reading palms. "He said my third husband would bring
me great wealth. I don't know how he knew I'd already had two
husbands. I didn't tell him. Did any of you tell him?"

She peered at the group but no one admitted giving out
Lucy's inside information.

"He told me my new husband would be a tall handsome
man from a faraway land," Jasmine said, tossing her hair and
looking meaningfully at Adam. "Why don't you go next, Adam,
and find out what this wise man predicts for your future?"

"It's not my turn," Adam replied smoothly, sipping his drink.
"We drew numbers, remember? Jay is next, then Sidney."

We were all comfortably seated with drinks in a pavilion in

the courtyard of the hotel. It was a beautiful evening, fragrant with the scent of flowers and a faint whiff of sandalwood incense.

"Okay, I'm next," Jay said, draining his glass and heading for the seer's table. "Hope I get great riches too. I could sure use some."

"He never has any money, does he?" Brooke commented as she took Jay's seat next to me.

"No, never," I laughed. "He spends every penny he can scrape together. He would rather have a designer belt than food. If his apartment wasn't rent-controlled he likely couldn't afford to live in Manhattan."

"Jay went with me and Rahim for a quick visit to the gem studio this afternoon prior to the tour of Agra Fort," she said. "I'm sorry you didn't go with us, Sidney. Jay really has a discerning eye. He helped me choose this amethyst pendant. Lovely, isn't it?"

I leaned forward for a better look.

"Yes, it's absolutely beautiful. You two chose well," I said, admiring the deep purple stone enhanced by an intricate setting of fine gold.

"Agra is known for bargains on semiprecious stones. If you change your mind and would like to go there in the morning, I think there will be time before we leave for Varanasi. All you need to do is tell Mr. Sharma. He can arrange a car for you."

"Thanks, Brooke, maybe I will," I said, knowing full well that my limited budget had no room in it for any jewelry buying, even at a bargain. That's why I hadn't gone along with them. I didn't want to be tempted.

"You should go," Brooke persisted, "Lucy and Jasmine each bought several things. Even Adam made a purchase. Now if that stingy Scot bought something, Sidney, so can you."

"Did he buy the jewelry for Jasmine?"

"I don't know. Perhaps. Now that Felix is out of the picture, Jasmine certainly seems to be trying to attract him. She was clearly on the outs with Felix. There was a quarrel the night before you arrived. Quite a public one. Spats involving Jasmine are usually pretty public." She laughed, her eyes dancing. "I'm sorry you missed it. She put on quite a show."

These glamorous people and their relationships were so convoluted. I wasn't sure I'd ever figure it all out.

Instead of shopping, I'd stayed by the pool after lunch with Justin. He swam laps for a long time while I read *Strange Gods*, Annamaria Alfieri's new romantic mystery, set in Africa. Her fine book brought memories of my last trip to Africa to mind, and the narrow escape I'd had there.

Finally emerging from the pool, Justin toweled off and stretched out on the chaise next to my chair. He brushed his straight black hair back from his face, took a long pull on a bottle of water, and said, "Ah, *merveilleux*. You see, at home I swim in the sea every day."

Justin was not a big man. He was slim, really fit and just under six feet, and he appeared to be quite strong. I thought the regular swimming might have had a lot to do with that.

As I sat with Brooke in the evening breeze of the courtyard waiting for Jay's fortune to be over and mine to begin, I watched Justin stroll smoothly around the pavilion. As usual, he was impeccably dressed, although the overall effect was casual elegance. I couldn't overhear his words, but I knew from other encounters with him that he always had a clever quip on the tip of his tongue. That these comments were delivered in perfect English grammar and in a heavy French accent made him seem even more sophisticated.

Justin chatted easily with one group before moving on to another, moving with the grace of an athlete or a dancer. Our friends were not the only hotel guests having drinks in the courtyard that evening; Justin mingled with everyone. Politicians call it "working the room." Watching Justin's polished performance, I thought he would have made a good politician. On the surface he was a really attractive man, but I sensed an underlying coldness.

Thinking of the afternoon's conversation with Justin at the pool, I suddenly realized that even after talking with him for over an hour, I hadn't really learned anything about him. Also like a politician, he kept his private life truly private without seeming to. There was clearly a public Justin and a private Justin. I wondered what the real man was like. I didn't think Brooke truly knew much about him either, for he had only been invited into the circle of friends a year earlier by Lucy, his neighbor at his vacation home in France.

I was just turning to ask Brooke more about him when Jay parted the curtains of the alcove and headed in our direction. From the satisfied look on his face, it was easy to see that he was pleased with what he'd been told. He plopped down next to Brooke and signaled the waiter.

"It's your turn, Sidney. You will love this guy, whether you believe in fortunetellers or not. The man is uncanny, an absolute genius, a true seer. How he can know these things is beyond me."

"What did he say that makes you think him so wise?" Brooke asked.

"He said a lot, Brooke. Good things. But the most remarkable thing he said was, 'You will always be unappreciated. It is your lot.' You both know how true that is, especially you, Sidney. Not at the agency, not anywhere. No one ever truly appreciates me. You see? The man is brilliant. Like I said, a real seer. Go. He's waiting on you. You're the last to go before dinner, I don't see Adam. Hurry, listen to what he has to say to you."

So I headed for the future waiting for me behind the tasseled curtain, my stomach aching from trying to hold in my laughter at Jay and his "fortune." I didn't dare look at Brooke. If I did, I would lose it. Always unappreciated. *Please*.

Entering the dim alcove, I took a moment to let my eyes adjust until I could clearly make out the little man sitting so still and silent beside the tiny table. The aroma of sandalwood was strong; it emanated from inside a brass burner suspended from a chain just behind him. The faint white smoke it emitted seemed to curl around his head, as if he were a genie. Small and ancient, he wore a shabby white robe and turban. His eyes were sharp and piercing under bushy gray brows in a brown wrinkled face. When he smiled, I could see that he had just a few teeth left. Those that remained were stained red with betel juice. A jar filled with money was the only object on the table.

At his gesture I sat on the stool opposite him, stuffed some bills into his jar, and somewhat reluctantly extended my palm toward him across the table.

Still smiling, he took my hand gently in his and bent over my palm, tracing its lines with his gnarled finger.

Expecting the usual patter about husbands and money, I was surprised at his silence, and unnerved when he placed my hand palm down on the table and gave me a searching look. His smile was gone, replaced with a serious look of infinite sadness and concern.

I couldn't ignore an eerie feeling that he had seen something in my palm that he did not want to share.

Finally he said, in a deep, slow voice, "You must be oh-so-careful on your journey, lady. One man has died on your path already. Others may follow. Evil surrounds you. But from the depths of the jungle, God will come to rescue you. Now go please, ma'am, go with God, for that is all I can say."

And then he rose, and turning, disappeared between the curtains behind him, taking his tip jar with him.

I sat alone for a moment in the scented dimness, stunned and frightened, wondering about the puzzling prediction that was not at all what I expected.

♓

By morning the uneasy feeling left by the fortuneteller was gone and I was feeling my usual cheerful self.

How ridiculous of me to be unnerved by the tiny man with the red teeth! It was all just an amusement, a parlor game to entertain the tourists. Everyone knows how these people make a living, right? The swami must have heard the talk of Felix's death and used it to scare me. And he had done a good job of it. It had worked well until daylight, when good common sense had swept the booger bears away.

I said as much to Jay over breakfast, along with a bit of an apology for being so moody and distant the previous evening.

"Oh, it's okay, Sid. I know you can't be Little Miss Ray of Sunshine all the time. I'm just glad you're out of your mood."

"It was silly of me. I can't believe I let it bother me so. In my rational mind I know better than to trust a fortuneteller. Nothing to be alarmed about, right?"

"Sidney …." he said, his brown eyes crinkling.

"Yes?"

"Just what exactly is a 'booger bear'? It sounds pretty bad to me."

"You might not have them in the North, Jay," I smiled. "In the South, booger bears are just about the scariest things ever for little children. They live outside, in the night, and they get after you if you're bad. You can't see them, but they're there. Sometimes they can even get after you if you're not bad, but are just in the wrong place at the wrong time."

"Oh. I see. So you want to try to steer clear of booger bears then."

"Yes."

"Okay. Well, we don't have anything quite like that in Pennsylvania, but if I ever come home to Mississippi with you I'll watch out for them."

"They can be anywhere, Jay, even in India."

"Thanks for the warning."

Following this intelligent conversation, we finished our breakfast and loaded into cars for an excursion to Fatehpur Sikri. After that tour stop, the plan was to go directly to the airport for a flight to Khajuraho, famous for ancient Hindu and Jain temples featuring erotic sculptures and listed as a

UNESCO World Heritage Site. Our bags had been sent on ahead.

We were travelling in three cars. Lucy, Brooke, and Rahim were assigned to the first car, with me, Jay and Adam in the second car, and Jasmine, Justin and Mohit following. Sharma said he had some personal matters—family business—to attend to so he would skip the excursion and travel separately. He gave no other details except to say that he would see us later at the airport for the flight to Varanasi.

Jay, riding shotgun next to the driver, was not particularly happy with our seating assignments, and Jasmine looked fairly put out as well when she saw that she would not be riding with Adam. I caught a flash of anger distorting her beautiful features, but it passed quickly. As we loaded into the cars she was already smiling and cooing to Justin in what Jay assured me was faux French.

Adam held the door for me as I settled into the back seat. Then he climbed in next to me and the car rolled away. I couldn't have been more pleased.

The journey to our next stop, Fatehpur Sikri, was not long, but it was long enough for Adam to spin several tales of his former travels in India. His stories were warm and funny, all told in his deep Scottish burr. I loved listening to him, but Jay didn't. At first he joined in the conversation, but the more I laughed, the quieter Jay got. Before long, there was no comment at all from the front seat. After a while I noticed that Jay was pretending to sleep.

12

～～～

"I T'S SO QUIET HERE," MURMURED Brooke, staring up at the magnificent pink and deep red stone buildings of Emperor Akbar's palace at Fatehpur Sikri, "I can hear the wind."

She was right. There was a profound silence in the place. I realized that we had become so attuned to the bustle of the cities crowded with people, animals, and vehicles that the splendid isolation of this solitary ancient site was almost a shock to the senses.

Mohit, again acting as historian and guide, began the history of Emperor Akbar, builder of Agra Fort and Fatehpur Sikri and grandfather of Shah Jahān. He gathered us round a huge stone tethering ring in the courtyard near the emperor's pavilion. There Akbar was said to have kept a chained elephant whose sole purpose was to crush capital criminals to death.

"In 1568," Mohit said in his sing-song voice, "Akbar came to this place called Sikri. He was twenty-six years old and still without an heir. Here he met a Sufi mystic named Salim who promised him three sons. The following year a son was born. So Akbar, in his joy, built this beautiful palace and moved his entire capital here, calling it Fatehpur Sikri, meaning City of Victory. But it remained his capital for only thirteen years before being completely abandoned."

"But why," said Adam, waving his arm in a wide gesture toward the five-tiered wind towers, "was all this deserted? It is magnificent."

"There was no water," Mohit replied. "The lake that was built was insufficient. Water had to be brought from afar, and after a time the effort became too much. So here it stands, abandoned. Beautiful, yes, but home only to the wind."

"Amazing," Lucy said. Shading her camera from the sun, she snapped shot after shot of the stunning palace.

At the end of the lecture we were given a departure time and then released to stroll at will through the harem and the various pavilions and palaces. The stone walls and pillars were elaborately carved in both the Hindu and Islamic manner. We were lucky in that we had the place entirely to ourselves.

I had envisioned a lovely morning, strolling through the palace with Adam and continuing the warm conversation that had begun in the car, but he was reclaimed upon arrival by Jasmine.

She entwined her jeweled arm in his and tugged him toward the harem. I thought sourly that it was not surprising that the harem was always the building that interested her most in these ancient palace complexes.

I soon forgot about both of them, however, as I walked alone from the Astrologer's Pavilion to the Treasurer's Pavilion, immersed in the stark beauty before me.

I wandered, lost in thought, taking tons of pictures even while imagining what it must have been like when Akbar was in residence. My imagination was really working overtime as I pictured the emperor sitting on silken cushions, counting all his wealth with his treasurer. I even thought I caught a glimpse of a man slipping from column to column in the shadows, where legend says Akbar played hide-and-seek with his favorite wives.

The silence really was uncanny. Mohit's resonant voice, the only one I could hear, soon faded away as I wandered deeper into the forest of stone columns, gazing upward in awe at the carvings of flowers, birds, lions, and elephants—mostly their heads and trunks. They were impressive even now, six centuries after they'd been carved.

I totally lost track of time. It was as if I had stepped back a few centuries. Sheltered from the blazing sun by the huge stone pavilions, lulled into imagination by the wind, I strolled deep into the sandstone complex. So deep, in fact, that it suddenly occurred to me that finding my way back to the cars was not going to be easy. I looked at my watch, realizing that it was almost departure time. There was no signage to direct me and I was not sure of the way out.

I decided to walk back the way I had come in hope of finding some of the others or an exit sign. I couldn't hear any voices.

I had just turned a corner for the second time, aware that I was seriously lost, when out of the corner of my eye I glimpsed a big man leaping toward me from the shadowed archway of columns.

"Gotcha!" Jay shouted, pinning my arms. "Surprise!"

My heart almost stopped. Catching my breath, I whirled to scream at him for scaring me, but then I could see that was what he wanted so I didn't. He released my arms and started laughing his red head off. I was furious, and my heart was still beating way too fast.

"Oh come on, Sidney, lighten up. I was just having a little fun with you."

I didn't say a word, just looked at him and turned to stomp toward the exit, which had been nearby all along. I wasn't speaking to the big galoot. I was headed for the car.

"Aw, come on, Sid. Didn't you have fun playing hide-and-seek as a little kid way down in Dixie?" he called after me.

No answer. I wasn't speaking to him, just marching to the gate.

Catching up with me, he tried again, this time with a pious tone in his voice. "You should thank me, you know, for making you aware of how dangerous it can be for a woman to wander alone in such a deserted place, especially in a strange country."

That did it.

"Thank you?" I screamed, "Thank you for scaring the daylights out of me like some big kid? Thank you? Seriously?"

"Yes. And that's just what you get, Sidney, for wandering off like that. I'm glad I scared you. Maybe it will make you think. What if it hadn't been me? What if someone else besides me had grabbed you and just dragged you off somewhere? What then? Better be a little more careful, Missy, unless you want to end up on a milk carton. If they even do that kind of thing here."

We had almost reached the cars. I marched on in stony silence and now Jay was huffy too, puffed up with self-righteousness.

The others were already seated inside the vehicles, with the engines, and more importantly, the air conditioners running. No one said anything as we climbed in and closed the doors. I was glad Jay was in the front seat with me behind him. Adam gave us both a searching look but said nothing as the cars rolled away.

♓

I apologized to Jay at the airport while we waited for the short flight to Varanasi.

On the long car ride from Fatehpur Sikri to the airport, Jay engaged Adam in conversations about Indian politics and economics, pointedly excluding me. Jay never made eye contact. I didn't either.

As the miles rolled by, I just looked out the window at the passing scene, tuning them both out. Finally I cooled down and realized that Jay had been right in his warning to me, even though his methods were childish and over the top. But what was Jay if not playful? His spirit of fun is one of the things I love about him. I owed him an apology for overreacting.

I waited for a chance to speak with him privately at the airport and found him seated in a Wi-Fi area tapping away on his laptop. He looked grim.

"Bad news from Silverstein?" I said, trying to keep my tone as light as possible.

He looked up at me and said, "Oh, hi, Sidney."

"Look, Jay, I'm sorry. You were in the right, not me. I've thought it over and I realize and appreciate what you were trying to do. I wasn't thinking. I was wrong to yell at you. I'm sorry."

"It's okay, babe," he said, with a little half smile. "Guess I was wrong, too, scaring you like that. Peace?"

"Peace."

He frowned down at his screen, patting the seat next to him. I sat beside him.

"Do we have a problem?" I asked.

"Yeah. You could say that," he said, turning the screen toward me so I could read what Silverstein had written. "Silverstein says forget about Sharma or trying to be tour directors and just keep Brooke happy, but that's not the trouble. The trouble is that apparently Felix didn't die of a heart attack after all. He was poisoned."

"What? Poisoned!"

"Yes. The cousin kept demanding an autopsy, so they finally did one. He died of poisoning. Some Indian poison, *cerbera odollam*, a toxic dose. Comes from the seeds of the othalanga tree. It stopped his heart."

"Oh, Jay, no!"

"Unfortunately, it's true. The toxicology report was conclusive. It took them a while to figure it out because it's hard to detect if you're not looking for it. But apparently quite a lot of people die of it in this country, often by their own hand. They call it 'the suicide tree.' The good news here, if there is any, is that Silverstein for once is not blaming us for stuff beyond our control. He just wants us to carry on as planned and keep Brooke happy and safe."

"Are you going to tell her about Felix?"

"No. Silverstein ordered me not to tell her but said we could talk it over with her later, after she gets the news. Sharma is telling her after his conference this morning with the authorities. That's the real reason he didn't go with us today. The police informed him about Felix and he had to go to the police station. Naturally, he reported to Silverstein without mentioning a word of it to us. He lied to us about where he was going. Remember he said he had 'family business' to attend to? Family business, my ass! He spoke with the police and Silverstein this morning and he is meeting us here at the airport for the flight to Khajuraho."

"That slick little weasel."

"Yes. I don't trust him for a minute."

"I don't either, but for once I have to say I'm glad he's running point instead of us, aren't you?"

"Yep. I am," he said, closing the laptop. "Let's go, Sidney, they're calling our flight."

⋊

Boarding at the airport was generally chaotic. Flights appeared oversold by a good margin. The boarding process seemed to be that all ticketholders waited in a holding area until the flight was called. Then, at the announcement, the gates were opened and there was a frantic dash for the plane. Seat assignments were a joke. People just grabbed the first seat they found, and when all were filled the door was shut and the plane taxied away, leaving the unlucky ones to wait for the next one.

We weren't part of the mad scramble because Sharma had showed up at the last minute and made a visit to the little room behind the airline counter with his black bag. The smiling, satisfied gate agent then ushered us personally to our seats on our small plane, ahead of the general melee. This was certainly not the normal experience, but with Brooke's money, anything was possible.

Sharma gave no explanations about his activities in the morning while we were on tour. He offered no words explaining his abrupt absence or informing us about poor Felix.

It didn't matter. Answers to some of those questions would be forthcoming. I had big plans to have prayer with Mr. Sharma at the first opportunity, as we say down South.

Before too long, Jay and I were seated aisle-across on a small, dingy airplane bound for Khajuraho. Jay's seat was broken and wouldn't remain fully upright. The seedy, smelly old aircraft certainly didn't meet the standard of Sharma's promised "luxury tour." I wondered what Brooke was thinking.

After takeoff, a flight attendant in a worn uniform came down the aisle pushing a tiny cart laden with small foil-wrapped lunch trays. She offered a choice of entrée, so I asked for the veg meal and Jay chose the beef.

He stripped off the foil, took a look at his food, and showed it to me,

" 'Look, madam, cow sits.' "

Then he tried to steal my lunch.

I wasn't swapping meals, but I did share mine with him. My food was pretty bad too, but it sure looked a lot better than his. I didn't think my meal would kill us, but from the smell of it, there was a good chance that his meal might.

"Speaking of food," Jay announced, "I decided this morning that I can stop being so careful about my meals. I haven't felt sick at all and I'm tired of being so cautious. It's boring. I had the whole buffet at breakfast and washed it down with a big glass of iced water and I feel just fine. I think I can tell just by looking if something is bad or not. From now on, I'm eating and drinking whatever I want. I think all the precautions we've been taking are unnecessary."

Following longtime travel habits, we had both so far stuck to our normal rules for meals where food safety may be a concern. That is, we didn't eat anything that wasn't cooked or peeled, and we drank only bottled water, bottled soft drinks, coffee, wine, and beer. No ice.

We are also pretty careful about buffets, where food might sit out unrefrigerated for too long or be contaminated by improper handling or insects. We never eat street food.

"Are you sure about that, Jay? You really think that's a good idea?"

"Yep. I think the danger of Delhi-belly is over. We both know that's not what killed Felix, right? And if the meal we just ate doesn't make us sick, nothing will."

"Do as you wish, Jay, but I'm not chancing it. I am sticking with the rules."

"Somehow I thought you would, sweetie. Always want to play it safe, don't you? What about that guy on television who goes all over the world eating weird stuff? He makes it okay."

"Only on camera. He's probably sick as a dog later."

"Well, I'm going to eat what I want from now on. Truly experience an adventure in the native cuisine. You know I'm a real gourmet."

"Whatever you say, Jay. Whatever."

I thought Jay was making a mistake, but I am not his mamma, so I let it go. And he was correct in that thus far on the trip we both had remained healthy and so had everyone else. Everyone, that is, except poor Felix. I just hoped the real gourmet wouldn't suffer the same fate.

13

~~~

I CORNERED SHARMA DURING COCKTAILS.
Rather than joining the group for drinks at sunset, I waited in the alcove outside Brooke's room until I heard him tell her good evening, close the door, and bustle down the hall toward the elevator. I caught him just as he reached it.

"Mr. Sharma, could I speak with you for a moment, please?"

"Ah, Miss Marsh!" he said, turning toward me with a wide grin, gold tooth glinting. "Of course, of course. I am at your service. Always at your service. However, I fear that I am very busy just now. I am late for another very important business meeting."

"Well, your important business meeting this morning with the police is what concerns me now, Mr. Sharma. Why were we not told the truth of the cause of Felix's death? And why did you lie to us about where you were going today?"

His surprise at my awareness of the facts showed briefly in his eyes, but he covered it quickly.

"Because I did not wish to cause you unnecessary distress, Miss Marsh. That is all. A pretty lady like yourself should not be concerned with these things. As I have told you before, I am in charge here and I will handle any problems that occur. Do not worry. Everything is taken care of. The details need not concern you at all."

"Murder is not a detail, Mr. Sharma."

"Murder? Has anyone mentioned murder? An unfortunate case of food poisoning. That is all it was. Such a sickness can happen to anyone in this hot climate. Unfortunately, sanitation here is not always what we wish it to be."

"*Cerbera odollam* poisoning is not food poisoning, Mr. Sharma."

Once again, the shock of my insider knowledge registered in his black eyes. They narrowed, belying his wide, toothy grin. I wondered if, should his body somehow disappear, his grin would remain, like the Cheshire Cat's.

"The toxicology report was wrong, Miss Marsh. A mistake was made by the lab. It has been corrected, just this morning. It now reads that his death was due to food poisoning. Salmonella, I believe, not suicide tree. Something contaminated that he ate. That is all. So sad, but nothing of concern to you."

Now it was my turn to be shocked. Was there truly a mistake? The poison of the suicide tree was said to be hard to detect. I knew that, because Jay had looked it up on his computer. Or had Sharma and his black briefcase somehow managed to have the report altered?

"I must go now, Miss Marsh," he said, pushing the elevator button. "As I said, I have an important meeting. Please go and enjoy the drinks with the others and do not give these distressing details another thought. It is all too much for your pretty head. All is well. There is nothing further to do. Do not worry. I have taken care of everything."

The elevator door opened and he entered, then turned and said to me with a sharp look as he pushed the lobby button, "But be careful, beautiful lady, of what you eat and drink from now on. Such an unfortunate illness can happen to anyone."

Then the door closed and he was gone with a wave of his pudgy hand.

☿

"I have to tell you that I hope Sharma's story is true," Jay said. "The last thing we need on this trip is a murder. We've got enough to figure out with Brooke's little puzzle. A real murder would sure complicate things, to say the least. I prefer Sharma's version. Food poisoning sounds good to me."

Jay took a sip of his drink, leaned his red head back on the sofa, and closed his eyes. We were seated in a quiet corner of the hotel lobby.

My first move after my little chat with Sharma had been to find Jay pronto and tell him all about it. I had snagged him from the cocktail party, knowing that I couldn't simply wait until after dinner to tell him the news.

"I know that, Jay, and I agree, but I also don't trust Sharma's word for one minute. I even think his little warning to me about watching what I eat and drink could be a veiled threat. What if he is somehow involved in Felix's death? He's sure working hard to cover it all up. "

Jay sighed, opened his eyes, and gave me his best benevolent grandfatherly look, which I hate.

"Sidney dear, I say we just let sleeping dogs lie in this case. The police are in charge. And poor Felix has his relative to go to bat for him if he's unsatisfied with the news. He doesn't need you. The case is officially closed. Chill out, babe. If Sharma and the police say that there was a mistake in the report that is now corrected, fine. Silverstein will be more than pleased with this resolution. Brooke might even be too. Nobody wants it to be murder. Nobody. Move on."

I didn't answer. He knew as well as I did that it was quite likely that the whole thing was a big cover-up, made possible by a wad of cash from Sharma's greasy black briefcase. We had seen it in action plenty of times already, though only behind hotel desks and airline counters, not with police or lab techs or whoever had made the "correction."

"Sidney," he tried again, "you know full well what Silverstein said to you before this trip began. Last chance, he said, remember? Do you really want to run point on this, knowing what you're up against? This is a brick wall, girl. There's no way you can undo that report even if you try. Do you think the Indian police are going to listen to you, a foreign woman, over Sharma? No. Give this up, babe. What will it gain you? Nothing. Felix will still be dead, the official report will stand, and you will be out of a job."

"But Jay—"

"No. We're leaving this alone."

He stood, straightened his jacket and brushed his red hair into place in a lobby mirror. Heading for the dining room, he added, "Don't be too long, sweetie, worrying over this. Just come on to dinner and put it out of your mind. It's the smart thing to do. The only thing to do."

But could I?

Long after Jay had marched off to dinner, I sat in that chair, mulling and stewing. Then I went to my room and ordered room service. I simply couldn't face dinner on the chance that Sharma might be there. I knew I had to get my head around it all before I saw that dirt bag again.

Plus, *nothing* makes me angrier than being "now, now little ladied." I can't stand the patronizing "Don't you worry your pretty little head about that" speech that I've gotten all my life when I've poked my nose in where some say I shouldn't.

My beloved homeland is known for that sort of thinking, but the mindset doesn't only exist below the Mason-Dixon Line. I had just experienced it halfway around the world, in India. In some countries, who knows what might happen to a woman who speaks her mind? I thought I knew the answer to that question.

After thinking it all out, though, I realized that Jay was right. I had to let it go. There was no other choice.

But from now on, I resolved, I would be on guard. I would be watching. And if anything else funny happened, I would act, no matter what it cost me.

14

JAY WAS LATE COMING TO breakfast the next morning. I went to his room to check on him and heard him groaning through the door. The hotel had thin walls and was nowhere near as nice as the ones we had enjoyed in Delhi and Agra. Perhaps it was the best to be had in the smaller city, or maybe Sharma was cutting corners. That would be no surprise.

I knocked on Jay's door.

A feeble voice answered. "Who is it?"

"Sidney. Are you okay?"

"No. I'm not. I'm sick. I think I may be dying. Please come in. I thought you'd never come. I need help."

"Well, open the door and let me in, then."

"I don't know if I can make it to the door. I'll try."

Have I mentioned that Jay is a big hypochondriac? The tiniest sniffle can send him into a tailspin. That's why I wasn't really worried as I waited for him to open the door.

When he finally did, I *was* worried, and I felt bad for doubting him. He really did look awful. He was beyond pale and had to hold on to the furniture to get back in bed. I could tell it was real this time and not just one of his dramas.

"Tell me what's wrong, Jay," I said gently, pulling the covers back for him to settle back on the bed. I was truly concerned. "Tell me what I can do for you. Do you want me to call a doctor?"

"No. I think I'll eventually be all right, but it's going to take a while. I spent most of the night lying on the bathroom floor. I was a fool, Sidney. I should never have eaten all that stuff."

I felt his head. His forehead was cool. He didn't seem to have any fever. I went to the bathroom for a damp washcloth and wiped his face, then straightened his twisted bedcovers. He lay perfectly still in the darkened room, groaning.

It was hot and unpleasant in the room. The dumpy hotel's air conditioning didn't seem to be working very well. I opened the windows, adjusted the shutters to let in air but not much light, and turned on the ceiling fan.

"I'll be right back, Jay. I'm going to get you something to help you feel better."

I usually carry this pharmacy in my bag whenever we are headed to countries where the Duane Reade is not on the next corner. Before long I was back with some tablets my druggist had given me against just such an occasion. I had powdered Gatorade as well, which I mixed with bottled water and brought to Jay's bedside.

"Drink this if you can, Jay. Tiny sips at first."

Before long, he seemed better, enough so that I was no longer alarmed. He said he was too weak to go on the day's tour, though, in the heat. I thought that was wise.

"Do you want me to stay here with you, Jay? I don't mind one bit missing the tour."

"No. You go on ahead, babe. I'll manage. I'll have them bring me some toast and tea later. I'm going to sleep now. I think that will help me most. I didn't get much sleep last night."

"Well, okay. If you're sure you'll be all right—"

"I'm sure. Really."

I turned toward the door.

"Sidney?"

"Yes, Jay?"

"Turn the radio on to some music, please. Some soft music would be nice. You may have noticed that there's no TV in this dump. Sharma should be ashamed, booking Brooke's nice tour into a place like this. Hope it doesn't blow back on us."

I fiddled with the radio dials. The best I could do was a local station playing sitar music.

"At least our agency won't be blamed for it, Jay. Brooke knows who made the reservations. Sorry about the music. It's not exactly Brahms's *Lullaby*, but it's all I can find."

"It's okay, Sid. Thanks. Have fun on the tour. Take some pictures for me."

I felt really sorry for him. I knew he hated to miss any of the exotic sights on the schedule. The very fact that he told me to go on without him showed how bad he felt. This was real. If he is having one of his swoons, he wants all the attention anyone will give him. When he doesn't put on a big show, it's serious.

I grabbed my camera from my room and headed down the stairs to the front of the hotel, where our tour van had just pulled up and was waiting. I was lucky that it hadn't already left.

"Where's Jay?" Lucy asked. "Isn't he coming? Oh, dear, I hope he's not ill."

"As a matter of fact, he *is* ill," I said, as Nigel hopped out of the van and opened the doors, "but not seriously. Something he ate, I think. He should be fine in a few hours."

Brooke shot me a sharp look, brows raised. "Are you sure he doesn't need a doctor, Sidney?"

"Yes," I said, "I think he'll be feeling better soon."

"Good. Rahim is not going with us this morning. I will ask him to check on Jay while we're gone,"

Justin made room for me on the seat next to him. Jasmine and Adam were in the back seat, then Brooke and Lucy, then Justin and me. Mohit was in the front with Nigel. Rahim closed the door, and we were off, bumping down the rutted lane toward the monument complex.

The Khajuraho Group of Monuments, built between 950 and 1150, was overgrown by the jungle and known only to locals until discovered by a British engineer and a British general in the nineteenth century. Today, Khajuraho is one of the most popular tourist sites in India and a World Heritage site.

The temple complex is huge, covering some eight square miles in its entirety. There were originally eighty-five sandstone buildings but only twenty-six remain in a fair state of preservation. The complex is divided into three sections. About ten percent of the temples are covered in erotic carvings. Those carvings are the main attraction.

It didn't take long to reach the temple complex, unload, and march through the gates in Mohit's wake.

The day promised to be another hot one, but there was a freshness in the air that morning, making me doubly sorry to have left Jay behind.

Mohit, standing in the shade of a purple umbrella, described the Chandela monarchs, builders of the complex, who preceded the Mughal invaders in ruling this part of India. He pointed us in the direction of each temple group and announced our meet-back and departure times. Then the group split up, with Brooke, Lucy and Justin heading in one direction and Adam and Jasmine in another.

I stayed for a while with Mohit, asking questions, trying to get a better handle on the Hindu gods. There are so many that it's hard for the uninitiated to keep them straight, even the main ones, but I was getting there. I really wanted to understand at least the basics in this ancient religion, which is followed by the majority of India's citizens.

He was pleased with my questions. He smiled, and through his thick round glasses, he fixed his intent stare on my face and said, "It is written, 'The goal of mankind is knowledge.'"

As was his custom, he told me more than I wanted to know,

though it was all fascinating. When he finally wound down, I thanked the curious little man, then headed down the path that Brooke's group had taken.

The architecture of the temples was different from any we'd seen thus far, reminding me of a jungle adventure movie. It was so exotic that I almost expected to meet Harrison Ford dressed as Indiana Jones on the path. I wished Jay was with me. I felt so bad for him, ill and stuck in the shabby hotel room.

"Are you shocked by these images, Sidney? Or do they please you?"

Justin's heavily accented voice startled me. I hadn't realized that he was standing there watching me, in the shadow of the Lakshmana temple. I had been wandering alone for a while, staring at the intricate stone carvings, some depicting explicit sexual life during medieval times. The one directly in front of me was X-rated, for sure.

I could feel the heat rising in my face as I looked from a carving of an exuberantly entwined foursome and a horse into Justin's smiling eyes. Those eyes raked my body as he stepped closer. I'm used to looks from guys, but this bold appraisal made me extremely uncomfortable.

"I've been waiting here for you to come along, *chérie*, so I could explain all this to you. I am an expert in such *objet d'arts*. Would you like to hear my explanation?"

He was now in my space and the silent invitation in his eyes was clear.

I stumbled backwards, into the darkened, cave-like entrance of the deserted temple, causing him to laugh. There was a look of triumph in his eyes. I still hadn't said anything, hadn't answered him. It was as if I couldn't speak. He knew how uncomfortable his movements and words had made me and seemed to revel in it.

A twig broke on the path and I could hear Lucy's voice chattering as they approached the temple.

Then Justin diffused the tension that had suddenly risen

between us by turning back outside to the carved wall and launching into a lengthy academic description of the process involved in building the sandstone temples entirely without mortar.

I was relieved. The dry lecture broke the spell and gave me time to regain my composure. I stepped back into the sunlight, but well away from him. I had no personal interest in Justin whatsoever and was relieved that the charged moment had passed so easily. This man was really smooth, not my type at all. I didn't really even like him and I did not trust him in the least.

There was something disturbing about Justin. I couldn't identify exactly what bothered me. He seemed to be a successful, sophisticated professional, but I sensed that there was something deeply wrong inside somewhere. Something about him did not ring true.

Brooke had told us that Justin came from an honorable, aristocratic family of vintners from the Provence region of France. Though she had only met him within the last year through his neighbor Lucy, Brooke seemed fond of him. And Brooke is usually a pretty good judge of character. Maybe I was wrong in my impression.

As he continued to talk, completely impersonally, I began to doubt myself. I wondered if what I thought had just occurred between us had really happened at all, or if it was just a product of an overactive imagination, brought on by the heat, the lurid carvings, and the strangeness of the setting. I decided my uneasiness might have been unfounded, an overreaction on my part.

Thankfully, Lucy and Brooke drew near just then, and Lucy's bright conversation and Brooke's wry comments about the activities depicted in stone made us all laugh. We started toward the exit and the van. I was walking with Brooke, with Lucy and Justin following. I could feel his eyes on my back and even though I knew it seemed silly, I resolved to somehow switch seats when we arrived at the car park.

"I wish Jay had been here this morning, don't you, Sidney?" Brooke said. "What a kick he would get out of all this. Let's see if there's a gift shop so we can buy him a book of photos."

"Or postcards to send to his friends," Lucy suggested. "although photos of these figures might not be allowed through the mail."

When we got to the meet point, Adam was not there, but Jasmine was, and she was angry. She said he had left earlier in a taxi. She was insulted, I think, that he apparently felt he had more important things to do than stroll through the sexually charged complex arm in arm with her.

I had wondered why she'd turned up bright and early to go on the tour when her usual pattern was to sleep in and skip the excursions. Once I saw the stone carvings I understood what had prompted her participation.

We didn't need to find a shop after all, for vendors were hawking all sorts of souvenirs near the exit. At Brooke's urging, we chose an assortment for Jay, then loaded into the van to return to the hotel for lunch. I was especially happy that the tour had not lasted all day, for I was really worried about Jay and didn't want to be away from him for too long. I had looked forward to this tour, but it had turned out not to be quite what I had expected, and I was glad it was over.

$$\mathcal{H}$$

Things had improved by the time I got back to Jay's room. He was no longer being brave. The "poor me" phase had set in, letting me know he was well on his way to recovery.

"There you are!" he said. "Thank God you're back! If the cholera didn't kill me, I thought the boredom might. I couldn't sleep anymore and so I just lay here, staring at the ceiling fan going round and round, wanting to die. The only sound was the swish of the fan and that terrible twangy music. I thought,

'This is not how it's supposed to be. I wasn't meant to depart this life lying in a cheap hotel in India, listening to sitar music, watching a damn ceiling fan revolve.' "

I laughed, "Well, I think you are going to make it now. You look tons better than you did this morning. Why don't you grab a shower? Then we'll get out of this room and have something simple for lunch. I'll just wait right here in this chair until you're ready. Call out if you need me, like if you start to faint or something."

He opened his mouth to say that he was too weak for lunch, but then had second thoughts, grabbed some clothes, and headed to the bathroom.

I know him so well. Seeing him, hearing him, I could tell that the swoon was past.

This illness had been real, though, and frightening. We were both relieved that it had not been more serious. No one was voicing it, but each of us was fully aware of just how bad it might have been.

Over lunch, with no salad, buffet or ice this time, I gave Jay the souvenirs that the others had bought for him. He was delighted. Because it was so late, we were alone in the dining room. The others had already finished lunch.

As expected, he loved the bawdy pictures and immediately planned who the recipients of the postcards would be.

He was not so pleased with my mention of my encounter with Justin.

"He came on to you, too? I thought I was the only one."

"Really, Jay? He hit on you?"

"Yep. In Agra. I didn't tell you because, well, just because."

"Because you weren't totally sure that's what he meant. Because he didn't actually say anything that could be used against him. Because he just generally creeped you out."

"Yes. Exactly. Don't like one thing about that sneaky dude. I think we both need to steer clear of Monsieur Justin from now on, Sidney. But he bears watching just the same. Sneaky. We need to keep an eye on him. He's just the type to turn out to be a poisoner. If he wanted to take someone out, that's the sort of sly method that would appeal to him."

By the middle of the afternoon, our little caravan was loaded up and moving on, headed back to the airport and Varanasi, the holy city of the Hindu, on the banks of the Ganges River.

15

"**P**LEASE TELL ME THAT'S NOT what I think it is," said Jay, staring at the prone figure of what appeared to be a woman, wrapped in white muslin cloth and covered in orange marigolds. The body was being carried in a small procession that had blocked all traffic, including our van, entering Varanasi.

The day was going to be a scorcher, and even though it was after the rains, dust lay thick on the road.

She lay on a bamboo stretcher. A pink sari was tied to hold the flowers in place, keeping the petals from blowing away in the wind. The corpse was carried high on the shoulders of a group of mournful relatives moving slowly down the street in front of us.

The sad little procession had brought what was already congested traffic to a standstill. We had been picked up at the airport by a large luxury van and were on our way into the city. The deceased was the first body we saw in Varanasi, but certainly not the last.

"Because this is a holy city," Mohit said, "people wish to bring the bodies of their loved ones to this place to commit their ashes to Mother Ganges, our holy river. Most of the bodies are burned on the crematory *ghats*, which are wide stones steps or platforms extending down from the city to the edge of the river. Soon you will see. The government built a crematorium there, but many people do not wish to use it and still prefer the traditional funeral pyres. For all time, it has been so. The waters of the Ganges cleanse the soul and guide the dead on the path toward heaven."

"You said *some* of the bodies are cremated," Brooke asked. "Aren't they all?"

"No, madam," Mohit replied. "Holy men, children, and victims of disease are not cremated. Their bodies go straight into the river."

Lucy visibly shuddered, asking, "Are there many of those?"

"Yes, madam," he answered, with one of his steady stares through his thick round glasses. "There are said to be about sixty thousand of those each year. We call them Ganga people."

"Moving on," Jay said. "Enough of this grisly conversation. Too much talk of death today. Traffic is breaking up ahead. Let's roll."

I agreed. Seeing the funeral procession had brought my thoughts back to Felix and his untimely demise. Poisoned! How could that have happened? How could he have ingested such a poison? Where did he get it? I had never heard of it before coming here.

"Ah, the fruit of the suicide tree," Mohit had said when I asked him earlier about the name of the poison. "Yes, yes, it grows in the South, the Kerala region. A lovely fragrant tree with white flowers and dark green leaves, but its seeds bring death. For this purpose, the seeds are ground and mixed in a spicy curry to hide the bitter taste. Many people die each year from this tree. Sometimes it is fed to young women who have brought shame on their families. Very sad. Very, very sad to pass to another life in this way."

It was unlikely that Felix had purposely or accidentally

ingested such a poison to stop his heart. Obtaining a supply of it to poison either yourself or someone else would be relatively simple, Mohit said. It grows wild in the marshy areas of Southern India, where its fruit and seeds are easily obtained. Even here, in Northern India where it did not normally grow, it could likely be bought in the street markets. Everything else under the sun was for sale. Why not that?

So someone must have either fed it to him in his food or drink or injected him with a concentration of it. Injection. That method of administration had just occurred to me. Did any evidence of injection show up in the autopsy report? I would have to find out.

It was possible that Sharma already knew the answer to this question. When we reunited at the hotel I would have lots of questions for that fine gentleman, though I was not at all sure he would answer them. His whole treatment of us thus far, and particularly me, had been so high-handed and sly. In addition to his lies, his manner had been extremely chauvinistic. I deeply resented it.

I remembered then that the poisoned candy at Brooke's dinner that had prompted this whole tour had also been injected. I would have to find out exactly what that poison was, if she remembered from the chemical analysis.

"Here we go," Adam said, "finally moving again."

The procession veered off to the left, into a side street, and traffic inched along before picking up speed as the way cleared in front of us.

In the city center, at Rahim's signal, the driver of our van pulled to the edge of the street, stopped, and jumped out to open the doors.

We crossed the dusty street, dodging people, cars, pedicabs, cows, and cow patties. Following Mohit's lead, our group entered a narrow, twisting passageway between centuries-old stone buildings.

I shuddered with horror and deep pity as we squeezed past

people suffering from the effects of terrible diseases. Each struggled toward the river at his own pace, all hoping for relief of some kind from the holy waters. Lepers, victims of elephantiasis, polio, and blindness, all were moving in a slow, steady stream toward the healing waters of the Ganges. Oddly, these poor people did not seem to be terribly sad, but instead, hopeful.

Rahim, now walking beside me in the narrow serpentine street offered this explanation: "For some, to die at the banks of Mother Ganges brings release, freeing the soul to heaven. For others, the waters bring healing. Tomorrow we will visit her at dawn, when everyone comes to drink the holy waters."

Varanasi or Benares, its English name, is one of the oldest living cities in the world. It is even mentioned in ancient texts and was first settled around three thousand years ago. Hindus believe it was founded by Lord Shiva, who is also known as the god of destruction. Shiva, one of the main Hindu gods, is depicted with a third eye on his forehead, a snake around his neck, and the holy river Ganges flowing from his matted hair.

Emerging from the shadows of the overhanging buildings in the narrow lane, our little group came to an abrupt halt as the sunlit river scene came into view.

"Astounding," Adam said in a low voice just behind me. "Absolutely amazing." I turned to reply but his gaze was on the panorama in front of us. Adam had spoken not to me, but to himself.

It *was* astounding, unlike any riverfront I had ever seen.

A teeming mass of people swarmed the *ghats*—the ancient steps—washing, bathing, meditating, with vendors selling candles and all sorts of religious objects. The canyon of the riverfront was lined with crumbling palaces of past rulers and temples dedicated to many of the hundreds of Hindu gods. Beyond the *ghats*, the Ganges flowed past it all. Everything looked terribly ancient.

"*C'est brun*," Justin said, gazing at the water, "I expected this holy river to be blue, not brown."

"It's the pollution," Adam said, "Millions of gallons of industrial waste and raw sewage are pumped into it every day. Yet the people drink from it. Look there."

He pointed to a man standing waist-deep in the swirling water. He dipped a cup brimming full, and held it toward the sky with both hands before draining it.

"Somehow, it doesn't kill them," Adam said. "Gandhi was said to have carried Ganges water with him on his travels. I expect drinking the waters would put any one of us in the hospital."

"Well, let's don't just stand here gawking in this heat," Brooke said. "Move forward, please, into the shade of that temple. Mohit can explain things there as well as here in the sun. Don't you remember what Noel Coward said?"

"I do," said Lucy, fanning with a little paper fan she had bought, "'Mad dogs and Englishmen go out in the noonday sun.' It's true."

The heat was intense, even in the shade of the temple walls, but I was so fascinated by what I saw before me that I'd barely noticed until now.

Mohit gathered us 'round and began a lengthy explanation of the pantheon of Hindu gods and the beginnings of Indian history at the settlement on the banks of the river at Varanasi. He pointed out prominent temples and palaces and said that we would see more of the ancient city, including the crematory *ghats*, from the river the following morning.

As he was talking, I spotted Justin pulling Rahim off to the side for a whispered conversation. With the end of Mohit's speech came the realization that Justin and Jasmine were no longer with us. Looking back the way we had come, I caught sight of Jasmine's bright dress just as the two of them disappeared into the alley between the temples.

Jay had seen them leaving too.

"Wonder where they're headed?" he said. "Guess she's giving Adam a little payback for dumping her at Khajuraho. I don't know if you've noticed, babe, but I don't think he cares one bit what Jasmine does."

I'd noticed. I'd definitely noticed.

"I have to say that bailing out on Mohit's spiel is tempting," he went on, mopping his forehead with his handkerchief. "He knows his stuff but it's hot and his long speeches are a lot to take in. I don't intend to miss the visit to the silk shop at the end of the tour, though. Brooke says it's fabulous. We go there next. Are you going to buy yourself a sari, Little Miss Tightwad? I think you should."

"Maybe. I've already bought one, remember? The silver and blue one? But if I do buy another, Jay, where would I wear it?"

"Doesn't matter. It's just something you should get as a remembrance of this trip. Maybe we'll have an Indian dinner party when we're back in New York. That could be fun. I already have my turban, but I might buy another."

Rahim led the way out through the maze of serpentine streets, murmuring "Look, madam, cow sits" when necessary to help us avoid stepping in a mess. This time Mohit brought up the rear, waving his stick and warning off over-eager salesmen.

We were almost to the van when Jasmine and Justin reappeared, joining us with no explanation. S.L. Sharma was with them. He was carrying his bulging black briefcase, taking charge of the tour, and full of his usual baloney.

♓

Brooke summoned us to her room that night after dinner. The new hotel had proven to be about in the same class as the last one, perhaps worse. For sure, it was not the luxury accommodation that Brooke usually booked. We speculated that the powwow might be about the class of hotels.

We were wrong.

At Jay's knock, she flung the door wide and welcomed us in. A room service table had been set up with drinks.

"Come in, my dears, please," she said with a wide smile. "Have a drink or some coffee, whatever you wish. Then make yourselves comfortable. We have a lot to discuss."

We chose drinks and took seats in the crowded room. The room was a bit better than ours, but it still looked like an American motel room from the 1960s, except for the exuberant Indian artwork and big ceiling fan. The fan was working hard to accompany the rattle of the air conditioner unit that wheezed away under the window.

Brooke switched the air conditioner off.

"There," she said, "that's better. Can't stand that noise. If it gets too hot in here, I'll turn it back on."

"Brooke," Jay said, "I hope you don't think our agency chose this hotel for you."

"No, no, of course not," she said. "I know who chose it. I'm afraid we may have made a bit of a mistake in selecting Mr. Sharma to make our tour arrangements. It is somewhat surprising. He came highly recommended by Felix, who often visited India on business. The last two hotels haven't turned out to be quite as expected, have they? But we're here now, so we'll just overlook the lumpy beds and thin towels and enjoy what we came to see."

Once again, Brooke had demonstrated what a good sport she can be. Brooke is a realist, not a whiner at all, and she makes the best of most situations. Her sunny attitude is one of the many things I admire about her.

"I asked you to come tonight to discuss our friends, not our accommodations. Have you made any progress in identifying who my nemesis may be? You've had a little time to get to know your fellow travelers."

Jay and I exchanged glances.

"I'm afraid we've made little progress, Brooke, beyond just impressions," I said. "We have gathered no hard facts thus far that might point to any one person. But I want to say that I do not for one minute believe that Felix died as a result of accidental food poisoning. I think he was murdered. I think the original report was correct—death by *cerbera odollam* poisoning. I believe someone somehow gave it to him, he died, and then Sharma paid to have it hushed up. Sharma must have bribed someone to change the report and declare the first report a mistake."

I told her about my conversations with Mr. Sharma.

"But why would he do this?" Brooke said. "Simply to expedite matters and not delay the tour? Or did he have a deeper motive? Is he protecting someone, and if so, who? And why? This is really quite puzzling."

"Brooke," Jay said, "who in the group has spent a lot of time in India? Who might have developed a previous relationship with Mr. Sharma? Clearly Felix knew him, for he recommended him to you. What about the others?"

She thought a moment before answering. Then she ticked off the group members on her long jeweled fingers as she answered.

"All of them have been to India before. Adam has business interests here and so does Justin. Felix did too. That's how he met Mr. Sharma. Lucy has come to Mumbai and Goa both as a tourist and to visit friends. I doubt she knew him, but of course, it is possible. Jasmine, as you know, lives here and is a native of India. So she certainly could have met him, though this is a big country with a lot of people. The odds of a random meeting between them are small."

She stood and switched on the old air conditioner before continuing. It rattled into operation.

"So I have to say that any one of them could have had a long-term relationship with Mr. Sharma," she concluded, again taking her seat across from us, "though I am not aware that any such relationship exists. I don't know if they were acquainted with him before or not. You'll have to ask them discreetly."

"And any one of them could also have just met Mr. Sharma and paid him on the spot to get the report changed," Jay said. "When it comes to money, I think his standards are pretty low."

"Unfortunately, yes," she replied with a sigh, "I believe you are correct."

"Brooke," I said, "did anyone else have a personal relationship with Felix other than business? Were any of the group friends with him socially?"

"Currently, only Jasmine and Lucy, as far as I know. Felix didn't have many friends. Though brilliant with facts and figures, he was not a likeable person. As you already know, Jasmine was his 'special friend' recently. For a short time at first Felix was absolutely besotted with her. She is known to use her body to get what she wants. But it wasn't long before the relationship cooled."

"Jasmine and Felix," Jay mused. "I still think that's hard to imagine. He didn't seem to be her type at all."

"I don't think she requires a specific type, dear. She has had many 'special friends' of all stripes. You may have read about some of them in the popular press. Most men are mesmerized by Jasmine, perhaps even all men."

I was thinking of a possible connection with Felix's death and the poisoned chocolate at Brooke's Valentine party back in New York.

"Brooke," I asked, watching her carefully, "do you remember exactly what the name of the poison was in the Valentine chocolate from your dinner party?"

She looked at me steadily, with pain in her eyes. "No, Sidney. I'm afraid I don't. It was nothing I was familiar with, the chemical name in the report. I suppose I should remember it but I don't."

"If we called New York, could your assistant read it and tell us?"

"No, Sidney, I'm afraid not, for I locked the report in my safe. I'll take a look at it when we're back home. I should have brought a copy with me, but unfortunately, I didn't."

At that point we seemed to have run out of good questions. We chatted a bit about other things, but Brooke had little else to share with us beyond a warning to tread carefully in making our inquiries. She gave each of us a long serious look as she escorted us to the door.

"Remember, my dears," she said, "this is no game. Be on your guard, as I am. I am fairly safe, especially with Rahim to protect me. You are far more vulnerable. Whoever was behind the failed attempt on me and perhaps the successful attack on Felix is deadly serious and may strike again. Your job is to discover who it is without putting yourselves in jeopardy."

"We need to go home, Sidney, go home, go home, go home!" Jay said as we walked down the hall toward our rooms. "We need to tell Brooke we're out of here and leave in the morning. This is impossible. We're not even acting as travel agents or tour leaders here, which we are trained to do. Instead, we're supposed to be her eyes and ears, bumbling around trying to figure out a deadly mystery without getting ourselves killed. We are absolutely not trained for that!"

We stopped at my door.

"Jay," I said, do you think this could all be a delusion Brooke is having? Could she be imagining the whole thing?"

"No. Not really, because she has the proof of the poisoned Valentine chocolate locked away in New York, remember? That's solid, I guess, though we haven't actually seen it and are just going on her word that it exists. But if she dreamed it all up, if this is all a figment of her imagination and Felix's death was just coincidental, then what we are assigned to do is even more impossible and ridiculous. She clearly thinks it's real and is spending a lot of money to prove it, including bringing us along to watch her back and find the perp. But if she's right, Sidney, and it's all real, we're in way over our heads and I think we should bail."

"We can't do that, Jay. We agreed to come and Brooke is

depending on us. Plus, Silverstein wants us here. He is fine with it. He sent us along, remember? Even knowing better than we how it would be with Sharma and all."

"But he doesn't know why Brooke really wants us here. She didn't tell him the real reason."

"True." I nodded thoughtfully. "But even if he did know, I don't think he would care as long as he's paid well ... unless we somehow get more bad press for Itchy. All he cares about is keeping one of his best clients happy. It's all about money with Silverstein too, just like Sharma."

"No kidding." Jay ran his hands through his hair as I unlocked the door to my room, a sure sign he was upset and worried.

I gave him a little hug.

"Let it go for tonight, Jay. There's nothing we can do about any of it tonight. We'll talk tomorrow after we've slept on it. Goodnight."

My sage advice to Jay didn't work so well on myself.

I couldn't sleep.

After tossing and turning in the hot room for over an hour, wrestling through the whole thing in my mind, I gave up on sleep. I flung back the covers, pulled on some clothes, grabbed a bottle of water, and headed to the hotel garden for a walk in the fresh air. I felt safe in doing that. Even this cheap hotel had guards posted everywhere to keep out thieves and intruders.

⛎

At the sound of heavy footsteps on the gravel headed my way, I knew I was no longer alone in the garden.

Escaping the stuffy hotel room, I had found my way into the starry night, told the night watchman what I was doing, and wandered along the fragrant path in the walled garden until I found a bench where I could relax and try to unwind. A cool and refreshing breeze swayed the trees and caused me to shiver in my thin T-shirt.

The garden was the only lovely thing about the hotel. Someone, perhaps a previous owner, had given some thought to the way it was planted and constructed. Even though it too showed signs of neglect, the flowers were still beautiful, and it was a restful spot to compose my turbulent thoughts. A million stars spangled the dark sky.

Hearing the man—it was clearly a man from the sound of heavy footsteps—fast approaching, I stood quietly and considered my options. I could step back into the shrubbery to remain unseen, or break into an all out run for the light and safety of the hotel.

But it was too late. He was there.

When I recognized the boogeyman as only Adam, I was weak with relief.

"Hello, there, Sidney," he said with a grin when he saw me, "what is your business out in the garden this late in the night all alone? Not a wise thing is that, aye?"

"I guess not. But it was hot in my room and I couldn't sleep."

He smiled as he saw me shiver, either from the freshening breeze or the relief, I don't know which. I knew he was right. I had been stupid, not for the first time or likely the last. Adam put his arm around me as he led me up the path toward the hotel. That was nice. I liked that.

"The wind is rising. Open the windows and shutters in your room so you can sleep. You'll be cool enough now. Let me take you back inside, lass. In the wee hours blighters may be roaming this lonely place. This is no place for a beautiful girl to be alone."

We climbed the steps to the hotel. At the door, he paused and turned to me. In the shadow I could not see the expression in his eyes, but the suddenness of his kiss and strong embrace left no doubt in my mind as to what I thought was his intention.

Then he abruptly released me, almost shoving me inside the door, saying, "Scoot now, lass. Go to your room and sleep. And don't be wandering anymore where harm might befall ye."

Then he was gone, back into the night, leaving me to wonder about what had just happened.

As I entered my room, I wondered even more at my strong sense of disappointment and about the abrupt, inexplicable disappearances of the brooding Scot who I found so attractive.

16

THOSE SAME STARS WERE STILL dimly shining when we boarded a little flat boat and waited to be shoved out onto the Ganges the next morning, sometime before dawn.

Rahim settled Brooke, Lucy, and Justin in the boat, then helped the rest of us board. Jasmine was not with us. As a native of India, she'd said the day before that she was quite familiar with the Ganges and had no interest whatsoever in the early morning excursion, preferring instead to sleep.

Leaving the hotel, we hadn't even caught a glimpse of Sharma. Mohit and Rahim were the ones instructing the driver. Sharma seemed to have largely abdicated his position as a hands-on tour guide. His business was making a pile of money out of this trip, but clearly he had other fish to fry as well. He did not ask us to take up the slack.

At the riverside, Rahim said that Mohit would accompany us on the water and narrate, so he would be waiting on shore for us to return.

As our journey progressed, I had noticed that Rahim was not quite as vigilant as he had been previously. He was still attentive in his guard of Brooke, but he seemed more relaxed once we left Delhi. Bowing to Brooke, he stepped away from the shore. Looking over my shoulder, I saw him deep in conversation with a group of other Sikhs. I thought I had seen one of the men before, but in the dim, pre-dawn light it was hard to tell.

Seated exactly where I wanted to be—in the middle on a three-person wooden seat between Jay and Adam—I couldn't help shivering in the stiff breeze off the river. By noon, I knew, the air wouldn't be chilly at all. It would be hot, and the sun would be blazing.

Adam took off his jacket and draped it around my shoulders. Then he put his strong arm around me, pulling me closer to him.

"There, lass," he said, "that's better. You're shaking. You need more clothes."

Yes! I thought. *Or fewer clothes. I'm liking this man.*

I smiled up into the green eyes, thanking him.

Then that annoying little voice of conscience popped up in my mind, scolding me.

What are you thinking, Sidney? it said. *Don't mess around with this stranger. What about your captain? What about him?*

What indeed? It didn't matter about my captain. I quickly pushed aside an image of another tall dark man. I had loved that man with all my heart.

But his love for the sea was greater than his love for me, and I wasn't interested in waiting on shore in Athens for him, raising a passel of children alone. So it didn't work out. And now it was over. I'd told him so the last time he was in New York, not long before leaving on this trip.

So shut up, I told the little voice, *and leave me alone.*

My reverie was broken by a jolt, a scraping sound, and a splash as burly men shoved our little skiff out onto the river. Then the shouted confusion gave way to silence, broken only by the sound of the oars rhythmically dipping into the ripples. I was blown away by the sight of the great river, with its dark water now lit by hundreds of candles floating on the surface. I knew I would never forget it.

Tiny papier-mâché or wooden images of major Hindu gods, painted in bright colors—red, yellow, orange—held the candles as they floated on the dark water. The tiny candles had been purchased and lit by the faithful and sent out onto the river, along with their wishes and prayers.

As the sky lightened in the east in streaks of pink, purple and gold, other boats joined ours. Birds flew overhead, and I could smell the smoke from the funeral pyres. Then the great sun rose, and we began to float slowly downriver with the current, watching the *ghats*, where hundreds of worshippers prayed, bathed, and drank the holy waters.

Jay has this thing for rivers. He has a goal of swimming in all of the famous rivers of the world and has been known to pepper his party conversation with stuff like "When I was swimming in the Amazon …."

Occasionally, health concerns, like the parasite bilharzia in the Nile, will deter him from full immersion. Then he has to settle for just going out on the river in a boat.

Jay had talked a big game over drinks back in New York in anticipation of bathing in the Ganges. I have seen this happen before. The more wine he drinks, the taller his tales become. By the end of an evening, you'd conclude from his stories of the Mississippi, the Yangtze, or the Amazon that simultaneously wrestling a crocodile while fighting off a school of frenzied piranha was all in a day's work for him.

Now, as the rising sun gave us a clear view of the murky, thick-looking water, I elbowed him and said, "Okay, Jay. Here's the chance you've been waiting for. Jump in!"

He peered at the water without saying anything. Then he gave me a sheepish look before briefly trailing his hand over the side. He wiped it quickly on his pants and squirted some hand sanitizer from his pocket on it.

"That will have to do for the Ganges, Sidney. I can count

it because part of my body was actually immersed in it. But there's no way I'm jumping in there. If I didn't get cholera, I might just bump into a body—one of those Ganga people."

At that happy little thought, I shivered again, this time not from cold but from horror. I knew from Mohit's talk that encountering a corpse in the river was a real possibility.

Adam sensed my uneasiness.

"Relax, doll," he said. "Take your mind from such thoughts and enjoy the morning." He gave my shoulder another little squeeze as he reclaimed his jacket. "Look instead at the sky, and the birds. The sun is warming us all. It's going to be a fair day."

Watching his handsome profile and strong arms as he lifted his binoculars to scan the *ghats*, I thought that it just might be a very lovely day indeed. I was looking forward to learning more about this attractive man. Because of that, and my loyalty and gratitude to Brooke, I again decided I had no intention whatsoever of going home. Jay could leave if he wanted, but I was staying.

From the front of the boat, Mohit raised his staff and began pointing out the significant buildings and important *ghats* that we were passing.

Lulled by his voice, I found that the talk of the dead turned my thoughts again to Felix's unfortunate demise. Not for a moment did I believe Sharma's claim of a mistake in the autopsy results. I was convinced that the first report had been the correct one, and that Felix was indeed poisoned on purpose, not by accident. Gliding along in the boat, half listening to Mohit's patter, I studied my companions. Could one of them have poisoned Felix? If so, who? And why?

Lucy, seated in front of me in the middle between Brooke and Justin, was again chattering away to Justin in French. Both of them had known Felix well.

Then there was Adam. I knew that the attractive man sitting so close beside me had shared mutual business interests with

Felix. I absolutely didn't want it to be Adam, and didn't think it at all likely that it was.

I remembered that Felix had handled financial matters, not only for Brooke, but for others in the group. Had Felix's sharp eyes spotted irregularities that someone thought best buried forever? Wasn't it likely that it was the same person Brooke thought was targeting her? Who would profit from eliminating both Brooke and Felix?

"I think we've seen quite enough, Mohit," Brooke said, tapping him with her fan, interrupting both his spiel and my thoughts. "Let's return to the hotel for brunch. The day is getting warm and we leave early this afternoon on our flight to Nepal."

"Remember to leave time to buy silk," Jay said. "Varanasi is famous for silk. I simply have to get some."

"We will," Brooke said. "A shopping trip is planned on our way back to the hotel. Mr. Sharma has arranged it."

"Probably his cousin's shop," Jay whispered.

At the word from Mohit, the rowers turned the boat and leaned into the oars, soon returning us to the launching site where Rahim waited with the van.

On the way back to the shops, my thoughts returned to Felix and the fact that I would need far more than mere suspicion to force a further investigation into his death.

How could I manage that?

It seemed an impossible task. But as we slowed to a stop, the answer popped into my head. At the first opportunity, I would ask Mohit for advice. He seemed to have the answer for all things Indian.

The silk shop was definitely worth a stop, even if it was run by somebody's cousin, and even if it offered a hefty commission to our tour guides for bringing us in. This "factory stop" featured beautiful silk at prices even better than we had bargained for in the market. I ended up buying several pieces of silk—not saris, just silk yardage in a rainbow of colors—to take home as gifts for my mother and aunts. My mother sews, and most of the aunts do, too. I knew they would be thrilled.

The bargaining extended to the shop as well, and by this time, I had learned how to do it effectively.

"You want a camel for the price of a donkey," the shopkeeper complained to me. But we ended up agreeing on a price, one far below what the beautiful fabric would have cost at home.

I was really, really tempted by a lovely length of ivory silk, but I did not buy it. Jay knows me so well. He immediately understood why I rejected the purchase.

"You can't buy that because it will get your mom's hopes up, right, Sid?"

"True," I said, reluctantly placing the exquisite fabric back on the shelf. "She would know I'd bought it to make a wedding dress and I'd never hear the end of it."

Instead I bought black, and planned to have one of the tailors on the Lower East Side make it up into a dinner dress when I got back to New York.

♓

After brunch I found Mohit sitting cross-legged on a stone bench in the garden, arms extended, with his hands, palms upward, resting on his thin brown knees. His eyes were closed in apparent meditation, but with this puzzling little man it was hard to know.

"Yes?" he said, without opening his eyes. "You seek the wisdom of Mohit for the answers that trouble your soul?"

"I do, Mohit. I absolutely do."

He opened his eyes, staring at me through the thick round glasses.

"Then speak, madam. Tell me how I may be of assistance."

Deciding that I was at a point where I had to trust someone, I unloaded on Mohit. I told him the whole thing, from start to finish, and in the end I appealed to him for his help and advice.

"The blood of this man cries up from the ground," he said. "I will help you, for I see that you are sincere in your belief of what is right. I will make inquiries in certain places. But you must not speak of this to anyone, for he who has killed may kill again. Do you understand?"

I nodded, not trusting myself to speak.

He gave me a brief smile, then closed his eyes, raising his face to the sun, and said, "Go now. When I have something to say I will seek you out. Go now and say not a word."

Feeling immensely better, I left him in the garden and went inside to find Jay and coffee. I was happy that I had sought Mohit's help and confided in the wise little man. Somehow, I felt that in the telling a great burden had been shared.

♓

"Suttee," Jay said. "That's what would happen to you, Sidney, if you lived here and your husband died. You'd just have to climb up on that funeral pyre with him whether you wanted to or not."

We were seated in the Nepal Airlines gate, waiting for our flight from Varanasi to Kathmandu to be called.

"Jay, they don't do that anymore. It's illegal."

"Well, I bet they still do it sometimes. Maybe in some remote village. What if they did that to you? What if the flames were licking your little toes?"

"They couldn't. They'd have to catch me first. I'd run away."

Neither of us seemed to be able to shake the knowledge of death rituals that we'd gained at Varanasi, even though we were by then far away from the river and leaving India with the group as scheduled for neighboring Nepal.

They were right when they said India affects you. I can't explain it. It just does. I knew I would never forget India. It assaults the senses, and somehow forever changes your life. I had only seen a small part of the vast country and longed to see more. I vowed to return someday.

But at present, I was tapping the airport ATM, preparing to practice the time-honored art of *baksheesh*, hoping that to the greedy, money can buy anything.

Before leaving the hotel for the airport, Mohit had pulled me aside and informed me that Sharma was willing to part with a true copy of the Felix's original autopsy report if I were willing to pay him a certain sum for it. He said Sharma would give it to me once we were out of India if I had the cash to pay. He would also guarantee its authenticity. It was Mohit's opinion that this time, Sharma could be trusted, particularly for a certain amount of cash.

Wanting to get my hands on that documentary proof of the true cause of Felix's death, I agreed. I told Mohit to tell Sharma I would raise the money and give it to him in Kathmandu, even though I knew it would blow a major hole in my funds. I knew that if I went to Brooke, she would likely agree to provide the money. But after all she had done for me, including giving me this luxurious trip, I thought paying Sharma for concrete proof of what had happened to Felix was the least I could do for her.

Over breakfast at the hotel, I had told Jay of my decision to stay with the tour on the side trip to Kathmandu and he had reluctantly agreed to come along as well.

Jay looked up as I returned from maxing out a withdrawal from the ATM, trying to gather enough cash to pay Sharma when he delivered the document.

I was just about to tell Jay that I had made the deal with Sharma when he began preaching a text I didn't want to hear. "I've been thinking, Sidney, and I know it's eating on you that we're leaving India and you haven't yet figured out who took out Felix. I know you. I know it's hard for you to leave the tour without us accomplishing what Brooke asked us to do. But what she's asked of us is crazy, an impossible task. It can't be done by amateurs, and only possibly by the police. You and I've been lucky so far. You've managed to stay out of trouble and we just have a few days left on this side trip before we head back to New York. So now you just need to give it up, forget about snooping, and stay safe for the rest of the trip. If you can resist asking too many nosy questions, we might escape disaster this time. Can you do that?"

"Maybe. But I'm not making any promises, Jay. I am convinced that Felix was murdered, and if Brooke is or was really being targeted as well, I'm still going to try and find out who is responsible, as she asked me to do. I owe a lot to Brooke. I'm not letting her down, no matter what you or Silverstein or anyone else says. I can promise to be careful, but I won't promise to give up in the time we have left. I know how to be discreet in my questioning. I won't take any chances. No one will know what I'm up to. There'll be no danger."

"Yeah, right," he said, gathering his things before boarding the aircraft. "In that case, you better start looking for another job for us. I think we might need one if Silverstein finds out that Nancy Drew is on the case again."

After that little sermon, did I tell him about my deal with Sharma?

I did not.

17

SHARMA'S CHOICE OF ACCOMMODATION IN Kathmandu went a long way toward redeeming him in everyone's book. The luxurious five-star hotel we checked into was totally splendid. Each of us had huge rooms, almost like suites, with picture windows that framed a wide view of the snow-capped Himalayas.

Kathmandu is a magical place, no doubt about it. It is nestled in a bowl formed by the surrounding mountains and was closed for many years to the outside world, giving it a feeling of Shangri-La. This country girl had to keep pinching herself to know that she was really there, in this fabulous place, that it was not just a wonderful dream.

We spent the first day on an orientation tour of the old city, with its huge medieval buildings, palaces and temples, teeming with crowds of people. All of them seemed to be in constant motion, riding bicycles and motorized rickshaws, hawking wares, and bringing offerings to hundreds of shrines to hundreds of gods. I had never seen anything quite like it. The exotic beauty of the colors, sights, smells, and sounds surpassed even India's. I was especially fascinated by the people, small, beautiful people, all hard at work under the huge watchful eyes of the Buddha, painted high on some of the buildings.

There has been a settlement of people at Kathmandu since the seventh century, and the very age of the stones seemed to seep into our bones. I'm quite sure Mohit would say that this sense of the ancient is from the aura left by thousands of departed souls. A more progressive ring of relatively modern buildings surrounds the ancient core city, known as the old city, but it is nowhere near as interesting.

Because the old city is a twisting, time-worn tangle of streets, difficult to navigate, we were deposited in Durbar Square, the main square, to get our introduction to Kathmandu on foot. Walking to sightsee is much easier in Nepal than in India, as the cows are not allowed to roam freely; thus we no longer had to watch where we stepped.

"Gather round, please, gather round," called S.L. Sharma, trying to corral the group. Everyone was too distracted, taking photos and examining wares offered by sidewalk salesmen.

Adding to the general confusion was the fact that there was an annual festival taking place in the city, the Indra Jatra, the festival of Kumari, the Living Goddess. We stood in the crowd just outside her palace on the edge of Durbar Square watching as a tiny girl, adorned with heavy makeup and wearing robes and a headdress of red and gold silk, rode by us on a massive wooden cart.

Her ancient cart, with giant wooden wheels, was pulled not by horses, but by teams of small, strong men. Once chosen, the *Kumari* is trained never to show any expression. She stared with heavily lined, strangely vacant eyes at the crowd from her perch in a golden palanquin as the cart rolled slowly across the cobbled streets, making a sound like low thunder.

"Why, she's just a child," Lucy exclaimed, "a tiny child."

"Yes, yes," Mohit answered. "In Nepali, *Kumari* means simply 'virgin.' This is the Royal *Kumari*, who rules over the capital city of Kathmandu. Before the dissolution of the monarchy in

2008, even the king came to pay homage to her once a year. Her festival continues for a week, with events day and night."

"Is she a Hindu goddess or Buddhist?" Brooke asked.

"She is considered to be the incarnation of the Hindu Lord Shiva's wife, Parvati, but she is always selected from a Buddhist family. She is chosen when she is four or five after passing a series of tests, but is no longer divine after she comes of age. Then another child is chosen to be the *Kumari*."

"What kind of tests?" Adam asked.

"She must be very brave, without fear, and never show emotion. This includes being unafraid when locked alone in a dark room with the heads of sacrificed animals, dripping with blood, and surrounded by the howls of dancing demons."

"Poor little bairn," Adam said, with feeling.

"No, no," Mohit replied. "It is a great honor for a family if their child is chosen."

Following a guided tour of the most significant spots, the group split up to wander freely and shop, with directions from Sharma on how and where to secure a taxi to return to the hotel on our own at a time of our own choosing. The group scattered rapidly. Everyone seemed to have something special that they wanted to see or bargain for.

Brooke declared that she had seen quite enough for one day. Lucy agreed, and Rahim escorted Brooke and Lucy back to the hotel. Jasmine and Justin were sidetracked by the jewelry vendors, who were loudly hawking both Nepali and Tibetan bracelets. Adam, Jay, and I left them to their bargaining and moved on down the street. The two men were not interested in the cart of unusual earrings that sidetracked me, so I told them to go on ahead and I would catch up after making my selections. Before I could follow then, however, Sharma suddenly appeared from the shadowed entrance of a café, pulled me aside and whispered, "I have made the inquiries of which we spoke, madam, and the paper you wished for is in my possession. Do you have the price we discussed?"

I stared at him, wide-eyed, then dug in my bag for the envelope of cash I'd set aside for this purpose.

He closed his fat paw over the money, counted the bills, and stuffed them in his pocket.

"It is as you suspected, madam, I confess it, and when the time is right this official document will give you the victory you seek. Guard it well."

From his briefcase, he drew an official-looking document, and after looking both ways to ensure we were unobserved, thrust it into my bag. I did not pull it out to look at it then, although I was dying to take a peek. Despite Sharma's precautions, I couldn't take the chance that eyes might be watching. Inspection would have to wait until I was safely back in my hotel room with the doors locked.

Jay and I spent the rest of the afternoon wandering through the labyrinthine streets, buying the most amazing souvenirs for very little money and trying hard not to offend anyone with our photography. But in such a place, the temptation was too much. Adam had stayed with us for a while but before long he left us, saying he needed to return to the hotel to check in with his office.

We walked until I simply couldn't walk anymore. Then Jay hailed a motorized rickshaw and away we went, back to our palace of a hotel for long, hot baths, drinks, and my first good look at the mysterious document I had purchased at so dear a price from Sharma.

18

~~~

B ACK IN THE PRIVACY OF my room, I closed and locked the door, kicked off my shoes, and stretched out on the bed. Then I dug the paper out of the bottom of my bag, where I had secured it under the various small souvenirs I had purchased during the long, pleasant afternoon.

Knowing that Sharma was not above cheating me, I was pleased and relieved to find that the document in my hand appeared to be the real deal. As far as I could tell, it was an official, authentic, notarized copy of Felix's autopsy report stating the cause of death as poisoning caused by ingestion of the seeds of *cerbera odollam*, the suicide tree. Ingestion of the deadly plant had caused his heart to stop. Since I was fairly certain that Felix did not purposely ingest the toxic seeds himself, I could only conclude that he'd been murdered. The paper bore an official seal, was signed by the proper official, and the date/time stamp indicated that it was signed and sealed four hours earlier than the phony autopsy report that Sharma had earlier tried to pass off as the official document. But that one had always looked like a fake. Jay said you could get a better one run up anywhere in New York's Chinatown.

This one looked real. Where, when or how Sharma had gotten possession of it was a mystery. But I didn't care in the least about that. This report clearly proved the true cause of Felix's death. Had Sharma possessed it all along and only produced it after taking my *baksheesh*? There was no way of knowing. Sharma was a secretive and complex schemer, to say the least.

I thought about going immediately to Jay's room to show him the report, but knew that there would be little time to discuss our next move on this, our first night in Nepal. I resolved to wait until later to show it to him, after I'd had time to think it all through.

We were scheduled the next day to leave Kathmandu for a short visit to the famed jungle resort of Tiger Tops and return at the end of the week. We had been told that our same rooms at the hotel in Kathmandu would be held for us in our absence. Therefore we were only packing a small bag for the jungle adventure and leaving our big suitcases in our rooms. I decided that it would be best to keep the precious paper I had bought from Sharma at the hotel rather than risk losing or damaging it on the excursion. Talking it over with Jay could wait too, I thought, until our return. Nothing could be accomplished anyway from deep in the jungle.

After locking the document securely in the safe in the closet of my room, I dressed quickly and ran down to meet the others for a small welcoming cocktail party. Drinks would be followed by a festive evening meal.

After a fine dinner accompanied by a not-so-fine folkloric dance show, Jay and I spent the rest of the evening getting pleasantly hammered at the hotel bar, accompanied by Adam and some talented people from *National Geographic*. You may think, as I did, that such top-notch writers and photographers spend all their time slaving away from some hot, miserable, bug-infested tent deep in the wilds, but you would be wrong. For here these professional adventurers were, sharing drinks and swapping stories with us at the glitzy bar.

I felt a bit like Miss Scarlett at the picnic at Twelve Oaks that evening. None of these men had ever met a Southern girl and all seemed brainwashed by the fictional stereotypes of magnolias and moonlight. It was a fun evening, to say the least. Adam was extremely attentive too. Leaving the bar, he asked me to walk with him in the garden.

On the secluded terrace, he pulled a tiny silken bag from his pocket, withdrew a lovely amethyst pendant, and fastened it around my neck.

"Oh, Adam, thank you," I said. "This is beautiful!"

"I bought it for you in Agra," he said, "I thought you might like it, lass."

After a long walk and quite a lot of kissing in the moonlit garden, only the stern Victorian morals my grandmother had pounded into me made me turn down Adam's invitation to spend the remainder of the night in his room.

It turned out to be a good thing, for had I been in the sack with the Scotsman when I woke the following day I might have missed the surreal stillness of the early morning's glorious pink light on the snow-capped mountains surrounding Kathmandu. I sat transfixed in my nightgown, with my window open to the crisp clear air, the silence broken only by the pure sound of brass bells that rang out all over the valley with the dawn, sending prayers to heaven.

I also would also have missed the spectacular row between Justin and Jasmine that took place in the hallway outside my room just before breakfast.

Hearing the shrieking and screaming, I opened my door a crack and peeped out, just in time to see Justin running down the hall in his tighty-whities with Jasmine pelting shoes at him and calling him everything but a child of God. In the South, we call that dog-cussin', and Justin was the recipient of the Indian version.

"I spit on you," she screamed. "You think I will not tell them all what you are, you son of a donkey? They will all know, yes, they will, because I, Jasmine, will tell them!"

Not wanting to be involved in any way in the lovers' quarrel, I eased my door shut, my shoulders shaking with suppressed laughter. My only regret was that Jay had missed it, for I knew how much he would have enjoyed such a spectacle.

After breakfast, Sharma gathered the group and gave us the plan for our short visit to one of the lodges of Tiger Tops, the famed jungle resort in and near the Chitwan National Park. It was to be a highlight of the trip, something we had all, even the most sophisticated of us, been looking forward to.

Everyone, that is, but Jay.

He had come down to breakfast late, bleary eyed and hung over. On learning that we would have to travel to the lodge on elephants because the river was flooded after the monsoon rains, Jay threw a hissy fit that would even have met Jasmine's standard.

I knew during Sharma's briefing that Jay was getting all twirled up over something, but he hid it in front of the others. Not until we went to my room upstairs afterward did I find out what the problem was.

"I am not climbing on an elephant, Sidney, and that's final. Not doing it. Not happening, no way."

Jay stood with his arms folded against his chest and his eyes shut like a big, red-headed child, as if by closing his eyes he could make the whole situation go away.

Jay is terrified of large animals, a fact that I learned about him early in our relationship. His phobia was confirmed on our disastrous trip to South Africa.

"You have to, Jay, if you want to go to Tiger Tops. You heard what the man said. The river is flooded. The roads are underwater. It's the only way in. We have a short flight over the mountains to the Terai—the flatland. Then we land at an airfield and are met by a truck from the lodge. The truck takes us to the river. Then we climb on the elephants and they take us across the river to the camp. That's it. Simple. And it's the only way in unless you want to parachute. There's no other way. If you won't ride the elephant, you'll just have to stay here by yourself. Because I'm going. I wouldn't miss it for the world. I think it sounds like the most fun ever."

He shuddered, and looked at me as if I'd just said I was going to enjoy eating a bowl of worms.

He moved to the window, staring out without saying anything, his back to me.

I waited and let him stew, saying nothing.

"Sidney," he said finally, still with his back to me, "knowing me as well as you do, I can't believe you are actually asking me to ride a wild elephant."

"The elephants are not wild, Jay. They're well trained. People do this elephant-riding thing every day in this part of the world. Asian elephants are trained from the time they are small. This is one of the things they are taught to do—carry people. They're tame and docile. My Aunt Minnie could ride one of these elephants."

I stretched out on the bed, pulling pillows up behind my head and waited some more. I didn't say anything further, letting him have time to work through it.

Finally he collapsed in the chair by the bed and said in a low voice, "Okay. I'll go. I guess I'll have to. The ride shouldn't last too long, should it? I mean, the river is not too wide, is it? Sharma said a small river. I think I can stand it long enough to cross a small river."

⊬

The river was not small.

It was wide, way beyond its normal banks from the monsoon rains. And the journey was not short, either. It took hours to get there, rocking on a canvas cushion set on a small, wooden, railed platform atop a huge gray beast.

Our small propeller plane had flown over the jagged snow-covered peaks of the Himalayas, the tallest mountain range in the world, to a narrow green plain called the Terai. Everyone was glued to the windows hoping to photograph the famous mountains, trying to spot Everest and Annapurna.

The Terai is a narrow, marshy, grassy plain straddling the border of India and Nepal at the feet of the Himalayas. It is a fertile region and along the river on one side, small villages of farmers grow rice, wheat, sugar cane, jute and tobacco. The farmers fight off nightly forays from the Bengal tigers and cloud leopards that live within the sprawling confines of our ultimate destination, the Chitwan National Park, formerly The Royal Chitwan National Park.

Once the playground and private tiger-hunting preserve of kings and maharajahs, it is now a World Heritage Site. Chitwan, meaning "heart of the jungle" is open to the public and tiger hunts are no longer allowed. In addition to the tigers and leopards, the jungles of the park are filled with lots of other animals. It boasts a sizeable population of rare one-horned rhinos, sloth bears, rhesus monkeys, and mugger crocodiles and is home to seventeen varieties of snakes, including the rock python and king cobra.

After landing on a grassy strip, our plane taxied, turned, and took off, headed back to Kathmandu. It would not return for us for several days.

Brooke had chosen not to accompany us on the journey. She said she was tired from our travels, had stayed at Tiger Tops before, and preferred to rest in the luxurious hotel in Kathmandu until our return. Rahim, of course, remained with her, and Mohit and Sharma as well. Jasmine's burly assistants, who doubled as her security guards, were left behind as well. Tiger Tops was quite used to visits by film stars and other celebrities, so her treasured privacy and security was assured.

"You will not need any of our services on this most excellent adventure," Sharma had said as we prepared to leave the hotel. "All is arranged. The most famous Tiger Tops staff will take care of your every need until you return. It is most luxurious. If you wish anything, even the smallest of things, you only have to ask."

The description of luxury in a world-famous place sounded good to Jay. The descriptions of the huge variety of animals, birds, and reptiles to be seen, not so much.

"You can look at all the animals you want, Sidney," he said. "Just don't ask me to go with you. I'll be at the bar, chatting it up with the rich and famous, or in the spa, having a massage. I'll look at your photos of the cute little animals but that's all. That's as close as I get. You know I hate nature."

Jay might not be actively participating in the jungle safaris, but he certainly looked the part. Following his pattern of costuming for the occasion, he was dressed like a jungle explorer in a movie and I fully expected him to trot out a British accent before the adventure was over. I'm sure he thought I looked shabby in my old T-shirt and jeans.

A large green truck picked us up at the airstrip and took us on the next leg of our journey. Everyone except Jay was in high spirits, enjoying the adventure as we bounced along a rutted road and lurched through mud holes until we reached a clearing where a group of huge elephants and their keepers—*mahouts*—were waiting.

Ever climbed up on an elephant? Ever climbed up on an elephant without any sort of mounting platform, ladder, or stool? Well, I did. In the patterned shade of a huge kapok tree, the *mahout* told the elephant to kneel slightly, and another smiling man held the end of the elephant's tail, bending it into a loop against the big beast's rear end. Then I was instructed to step onto the big curved tail and clamber up. I couldn't believe it, but I did as I was told and it worked. It was actually easy. There I was, in two minutes, sitting on top of the elephant. And the elephant hadn't seemed to mind in the least. That mounting method was apparently routine for him.

Jay was still standing, ashen, on the ground, refusing to

mount the elephant. I thought it might take a block and tackle to lift him. He looked in no state to scramble up the giant gray rump.

But before long, seeing all the others mounted, he knew he had little choice. So he relented and was soon sharing my *howdah* with me as the elephant rose to full height and lumbered off, following the others across the marshy plain toward the river.

The *howdah* was a simple, practical device made a bit more comfortable by square gray canvas cushions. It was nothing like the heavy, ornate gilt conveyances commonly used in ceremonial parades.

Each turbaned *mahout*, riding just in front of us behind the elephant's head, guided the creature with vocal commands aided by his bare feet and a long metal hook. He was not seated on our rough wooden platform with us, but rather directly in front on the back of the animal's neck. He handed us two large umbrellas to shelter from the sun as necessary.

"I think I'm going to be sick," Jay said. "This is the worst thing I've ever done in my life. I want to go home. I want to go back to New York."

I glanced at him, briefly concerned that he might actually have motion sickness from the undulating gait of the elephant, but his color was returning and he looked fine.

"You'll be all right soon, Jay, once you get used to it. I think it's fun. What a view from up here! Isn't it beautiful? Look, there's the river!"

"We can't cross that, Sidney. Look at it. It's too deep, and the water is moving too fast."

But cross it we did. It was a piece of cake for the elephants. Apparently fording the deep swirling waters was routine for them. In no time at all we were through the water and slowly threading our way single file through the giant cane and tall, elephant grass on the other side. The white plumes of the plants, shoulder high to the animals, gleamed in the sun and swayed with the wind as we passed through. It was a beautiful sight. We were surrounded by a sea of shining white, stretching as far as I could see toward the distant shade of the forest of sal trees.

The ride was long. It took several hours, and well before we entered the jungle camp Jay's conversation had switched from his fear of the elephant to complaints about the discomfort of the *howdah*. We were both a bit sore and stiff and relieved to spot the dismounting platforms at the camp, where white-clad, turbaned staff waited to greet us and help us unload. There was no "Welcome to Tiger Tops" signage at the camp entrance, which was disappointing to Jay, who had asked me to take a picture of him atop the elephant in his ridiculous outfit to show off to his friends.

We were welcomed with drinks and a long speech from the khaki-clad manager. Then we were led down a series of paths to our rooms, in individual huts.

The quality of the accommodations was surprisingly poor, to say the least, for a place of such international renown. But at that point, I didn't care. I was just glad to be able to stretch out on the sagging cot in my tiny hut for a rest before dinner. The manager had said that a bell would ring to call us to the table.

When I woke at the sound of the bell, I found that my bag had not been delivered to my room as promised. I opened the door to see if it had been left outside. No bag. Annoyed, I ran my fingers through my tangled hair in the cheap metal bathroom mirror. I washed my face as best I could in the thin stream of water running into the rust-stained sink, and dried it on one of the small mismatched towels. Then I headed down the path, following signposts to the center pavilion, where dinner was waiting. I saw no other guests. The members of our little group appeared to be the only visitors.

The dining pavilion was actually another hut, about ten feet wide and fifteen feet long, dominated by a locally made wooden trestle table and benches. It was not air conditioned, which was okay in the cool of the evening, but I knew that in the heat of the day it would be sweltering.

I was apparently the last to arrive at dinner. Everyone looked up as I opened the screen door and slid into a seat on the bench next to Lucy. No one looked happy.

"I fell asleep," I said. "Sorry I'm late."

"It's fine, dear," Lucy said. "Dinner's late too."

Dinner, when it came, consisted of large bowls of rice and beans, fresh bread and farmer cheese, and a platter of sliced fresh fruit, all served family style. It was a good simple meal but certainly not the gourmet delights advertised by the world-famous Tiger Tops. It had become abundantly clear to all of us by this time that we were not at Tiger Tops at all. We were not sure where we were. Actually, the only thing that was certain was that Sharma had let us down again.

After dinner we sat in a circle of wooden and canvas sling-back chairs with lukewarm bottles of water and local beer, venting and deciding what to do.

Adam spoke first. "I had a bit of a conference with the lad in charge here. As you all realize by now, this is certainly not Tiger Tops. This place is called Big Tiger Watch Camp. They have similar activities, such as the elephant safari scheduled for the crack o' dawn, but I think the similarity to the type of camp we were expecting ends there. We are not actually inside the boundaries of Chitwan National Park either, but rather on the border of it."

"Can we leave this place in the morning and move to the real Tiger Tops?" Justin asked.

"I'm afraid not," Adam said. "I was allowed to pay for a call there, using the only telephone in the camp, in the manager's office. The real Tiger Tops is fully booked, and has been for some time. They have no record of any reservations for our group ever being made there at all."

"Did you try to call this cheap crook Sharma?" Jasmine asked. "I cannot stand this terrible place. Jasmine does not sleep on cots."

"I tried, but couldn't reach him. He did not answer," Adam

said. "I left a message for him to call. I don't expect we'll hear from him."

"Can't you call your man in New York on your smartphone, Jay?" Lucy asked.

"No," he replied. "It doesn't work. I tried. No signal."

"What about Brooke?" Justin asked. "Should we call her?"

"Brooke will be very distressed to learn what has happened, and she's not feeling well," Adam said. "I don't think we should bother her with this. The visit is short. I think we should just make the best of it. It's disappointing, but the animal viewing is worth the journey, and spending a few days in this camp is certainly bearable."

Jay stood and started pacing the circle, running his fingers through his red hair.

"Look everyone," he said, finally, "Sidney and I are really sorry everything hasn't worked out as it should with all the accommodations on this trip, aren't we, Sidney?"

I nodded.

"We both want you to know that we and our agency had nothing whatsoever to do with the reservations. Everything was done before we were ever brought into the picture. It has been professionally frustrating for us the entire time because the whole deal has been totally out of our hands. Sharma made all the arrangements and Sharma has been completely in charge, not us. We were told to back off. Our agency was brought on board by Brooke at the last minute. Brooke paid fully in advance for the very best and that is what she should have received, but clearly hasn't in every stop. For that, Sharma is responsible. Sharma did it all. But we still feel terrible and somehow responsible, especially for bringing you all this way to this Fake Tops."

"I must leave this place," Jasmine said in her dramatic way. "I cannot stay here. I cannot bear it. I must go back to Kathmandu."

"Well, you can't," Justin said. "*C'est impossible*. None of us can leave until the next plane arrives, as scheduled, on Thursday."

"Adam is right. We just make the best of it," Lucy said, with her pleasant smile. "It's not fancy, but it's clean, and luxury is not what we came for anyway. We came to see the animals. Let's just go on the elephant safari in the morning as planned. It's not really so bad here, just not what we expected. The food is plain, but at least it is edible, quite healthy actually, and the employees are friendly."

"I agree with Lucy," I said, speaking up for the first time. "After all, the jungle adventure is really what we came for, right?"

"Wrong," Jay said. "I wasn't planning on setting foot in the jungle. I was just going to relax at the resort while you did, and maybe have a massage."

"Well there's certainly no spa here," Adam said. He took a long pull on his beer, set the bottle down, stood and stretched. "I'm headed for bed. It's late and dawn comes early. See you all in the morning."

When I returned to my room, my bag was waiting for me. Nothing appeared to be missing.

Had the bag been searched? I couldn't tell, but I was happy in knowing that my newly purchased proof of Felix's murder was safely locked away in my room in Kathmandu.

19

MORNING BROUGHT MORE FRESH BREAD, a bowl of oatmeal in the dining hut, and some welcome hot coffee.

Then we climbed back up on the elephants and headed into the forest, looking for tigers. In years past, we had been told, goats were staked out as bait to attract the huge nocturnal hunters, but this was no longer done thanks to the efforts of animal rights groups.

I was happily paired on an elephant with Adam. We were in the lead, laughing and chatting. I really liked this Scotsman, and he seemed to be growing increasingly fond of me as well. Jasmine and Jay were next on the trail behind us, followed by Lucy and Justin.

Jasmine totally hated the elephant camp and Jay was making no attempt to soothe the temperamental actress. Their griping was loud and tiresome. Jasmine had not wanted to go with us on the elephant safari, but she did not want to remain in camp by herself either. It was the same with Jay, and I was getting a little worn out with hearing both of them constantly complaining.

"Look," I told him after breakfast, walking down the dirt path toward the elephants, "why don't you at least try to have fun? This elephant safari is a once-in-a-lifetime experience. You've never done this before and likely never will again. Think how great it will be to tell your pals. I know you are nervous, but it'll be okay. Since you're stuck here for a few days, you might as well make the best of it. It is what it is."

"What it *is* stinks," he replied, his lower lip jutting out in a pout. "I can't wait to get my hands on that fat rascal Sharma. If I hadn't thought we were going to the real Tiger Tops, as promised, I would never have left Kathmandu. If he hadn't screwed us up, I would be at a famous place where I could do something besides ride elephants. My friends want to hear about Tiger Tops, not Fake Tops. You think anyone would be impressed by this? No way."

I ignored him after that and was delighted when the *mahout* loaded me onto the elephant with Adam, instead of with Jay. Adam's warm smile suggested that he was pleased as well. I wondered if he had bribed someone to make it happen. It seemed likely.

The morning light filtering in thin golden shafts through the tall sal trees was beautiful as we entered the path leading into the jungle forest. The air was cool and fresh. As we moved deeper into the thicket, away from the camp, everyone fell silent. The only sounds were the birds and the faint sounds of the elephant's steps, muffled by a thick mat of decaying vegetation on the forest path.

The elephant's footsteps were clearly audible only when we crossed an occasional wooden bridge over a stream. Then dull thuds were heard. The well-trained animals clearly knew exactly where they were going and required little urging from the *mahouts*.

Everyone except the sulking Jasmine was eagerly scanning the underbrush, searching for tigers. Even Jay was watching intently. Most of us searched because we wanted to see the magnificent animals. Jay searched because he did *not* want to see them. The protective coloration of the great striped beasts helped them stay concealed in the dappled light of the forest.

The Bengal tiger, the largest species among the cats, once numbered in the thousands. Sadly, the tiger is now officially an endangered species, and less than two thousand five hundred remain in the wild. Like the rhino, tigers are aggressively hunted by poachers for their body parts, which are sold for use in the making of traditional Chinese medicines, and for their distinctive striped skins. They also face a threat from diminishing habitat. In the Terai, a constant battle is waged between the tiger and farmers, where tigers pose a threat to farm animals and occasionally humans. Bengal tigers can become man-eaters. In the last thirty years, we were told, thirteen people had been killed and eaten in the Chitwan and its environs. Jay loved that fun little fact.

A rustling in the underbrush ahead of us on our left halted our column, but it proved to be only a feral pig, rooting around in the bushes, not a tiger.

"The tiger's not close," Adam whispered in my ear, "or he'd be having bacon for breakfast."

A few minutes later a small herd of sambar deer broke into a run near the path. They crashed along the forest floor, leaping over fallen trees and branches. The *mahouts*, who had been riding along serenely, seemingly paying little attention to the sounds of the forest, were suddenly alert and watching.

"Our tiger might be there," Adam whispered, pointing toward a dense stand of giant cane. "Something spooked those deer."

Sure enough, doubling back, the *mahout* steered our elephant off the path to the edge of a stream. He silently pointed to the fresh mark of a giant pug in the mud alongside it. I took a photograph of the paw print using my zoom lens. No one was getting down from the safety of the elephants to examine it.

The elephant is not afraid of the tiger, or of any other beast in the jungle. Its familiar size and smell mask that of the humans riding it, and thus it is the perfect conveyance for such a safari. Plus, they can easily go in areas where a vehicle cannot, where if might be unsafe for a man to walk. Asian elephants, unlike African elephants, are easily trained and have been widely used for work and transportation for generations.

I felt safe on the back of the elephant. I could see from Jay's face and rigid posture that he totally did not, and was near panic. Jasmine seemed to have her hands full in trying to calm him. Having grown up in the Kerala region of India, she had been around tigers her entire life. She was not frightened at all, only annoyed at being forced out of her comfort zone.

We searched the jungle for quite a long time, but no actual tiger was seen, only his paw prints. Then, leaving the forest, the *mahouts* headed us into the marsh in search of another endangered species, the rare one-horned rhinoceros.

This time we were lucky. We found one deep in the marsh, placidly grazing. From the safety of the elephant, we rode quite close to the animal, close enough to hear the sounds it made as it munched the tender reeds.

After allowing enough time for everyone to see and photograph the rhinoceros, the *mahouts* turned the elephants back toward camp.

"Do you think we should explore a return to Kathmandu tomorrow morning rather than staying here until Thursday?" Adam asked quietly as we left the marsh and proceeded back on the path toward camp. "This morning has been terrific, but I understand that the program is the exact same each day and there is nothing at all to do after the morning safari except to enjoy the comforts of the camp. There is no afternoon or evening program. If we stay the allotted time, we may have a mutiny."

He nodded back toward Jasmine and Jay.

"It's fine with me if we return," I said, turning to face him after glancing back over my shoulder at the clearly unhappy pair. "I know Jay would vote to go in a heartbeat. But how can we? The plane won't be coming for us until Thursday."

"I've been thinking about that," he said. "I could call from the camp office to Kathmandu and arrange for someone to come overland and pick us up. If the others want to stay the full time, they may do so. But I, for one, am ready to return. There is business that I should deal with in Kathmandu. I wouldn't have missed this experience, but now that I have done it I am ready to move on. I think the chances of actually seeing a tiger are remote."

"How would we get there? Overland through the mountains?"

"Yes. The plane won't come until scheduled, but there are passable roads, though the trip will likely take most of the day. We'll have to cross the river first, so we'll need to make an early start."

I thought about it. Adam was right. Each day in this most basic little camp would be the same. I knew that the thrill of a couple of hours of elephant safari would pale quickly against the boredom of sitting around the hot little camp all the rest of the day for two days with nothing to see and nothing to do. Neither was I looking forward to a continual battle for sleep in my moldy, uncomfortable hut. Plus, time was running short until our return to New York. Adam's plan would give us extra time in the fascinating city of Kathmandu and give me time to present my precious document to the authorities. I was beginning to realize that solving this mystery might be beyond my powers, but bolstered by the true autopsy report, together with Brooke's backing, I might be able to get an official inquiry started. I was also truly worried about Brooke, and felt a strong urge to return and check on her.

"Count me in," I said. "Jay too. I won't leave without him."

"Don't say anything to him or the others just yet, lass," Adam said with a smile. "Let me see what I can arrange, first. It may not be possible, or there may be only one car available to come for us. In that case there would only be room for the three of us plus the driver, not the others, so they would have to stay here for the duration. However, from what I'm hearing, some of them might prefer that anyway and not want to cut this visit short. Mum's the word, doll. If I can manage a return for us through the mountains, I'll take you to the festival tomorrow night in the old city."

I liked that idea!

Thinking over Adam's plan, I felt relief. A vague sense of impending danger had been building inside me ever since we had first arrived in the Terai. I had no explanation for it. Who knew whether it was due to the roar of the tiger heard during the night, or just fatigue and physical discomfort? I couldn't pinpoint the vague feeling of unease, of malice. But it was real, and growing. Though the game viewing was fascinating, I felt an inexplicable urge to move on, away from this grim little camp. After the morning ride, the day would be long, boring, and hot. I decided that I would be more than happy to cross the mountains with Adam and return to Kathmandu.

♓

"Leaving? We're leaving early? No kidding? Sidney, that's great! I can't believe it. That's the best news I've had since we arrived here at Fake Tops."

I had found Jay sulking in a hammock and was pleased to give him the update. He immediately sat up, with a wide grin. "How did you manage it, Sidney? I thought we were stuck here until Thursday."

"Adam did it, not me. You can thank him. He called some business associate in Kathmandu and arranged for us to be picked up ahead of schedule."

"What about the others? Are they going as well or staying here?"

"I don't know. Adam said that he will tell them we plan to leave in the morning and see what they intend to do. There is a car available if they want it. But even though they are really wealthy, they are also really cheap, and may balk at the unexpected expense. I understand it will be quite expensive and Brooke won't be paying for the cars. I was worried about that because we sure don't have any spare cash, but Adam will not hear of us paying anything. He said he is going anyway and we are welcome to come along with him for free."

"Even better," Jay said. "I'm out of here. What do you really think the others will do?"

"I don't have a clue, Jay. They may not even *want* to go. Neither Justin nor Lucy seems to mind the lack of amenities. They have adjusted and right now are drinking beer and playing gin under a tree. Lucy told me that she found it refreshing to live so simply and wished she could stay longer. Who knows what they'll do?"

"Jasmine doesn't feel that way. I can tell you that for a fact. She hates this place. Won't she want to leave with us?"

"Jasmine has already gone, Jay. She slipped away early this morning, right after we returned from the elephant safari, without telling any of us."

"Really? How?"

"On an elephant, back to the other side of the river, where she'll be picked up and taken back to Kathmandu. She pitched a fit in the office and they arranged for someone to take her. If we go with Adam we'll do the same thing in the morning."

"Not another elephant ride!"

"Yes, big chicken. If you want to leave you have to ride the elephant back across the river to the road. We 'elephanted' in and we have to 'elephant' out. You saw that river. The roads are flooded. There's no other way."

⌘

By the time the sun rose the next day we were well on our way, back through the forest and marsh, bound for the river on the back of our great gray taxi.

Crossing the rushing water was not as scary as it had been the first time, and I realized how this unusual mode of travel could become commonplace to these people. Some of them depended on the elephant for work and transportation, much like the cowboys and prairie farmers of the Old West depended on the horse.

As before, the journey out to the road took several hours, but even Jay had grown accustomed to it. He was happy to be leaving so his whining had pretty much stopped. The two of us shared an elephant, following Adam, who rode alone behind his *mahout*. As predicted, Lucy and Justin had elected to remain behind and Jasmine was long gone. We would all be reunited eventually in Kathmandu with Brooke.

A small green car was waiting for us in the clearing under the kapok tree, and a small, smiling man stood beside it.

The elephants stopped, and at the command of the *mahouts*, knelt down so we could dismount, again using the elephant's tail as a step.

As we slid to the ground, the man with the car rushed up to us and bowed, palms together in a traditional Hindu greeting. "Good morning lady and gentlemen. I am here as ordained to take you to Kathmandu. I am Shiva, god."

"Well, Sidney," Jay said, laughing, as Shiva held the car door for us to climb in, "your swami's prophecy came true. 'From the depths of the jungle,' a god came to rescue you."

The overland journey through the Himalayas was thrilling, to say the least, particularly as the road was a narrow two-lane at best. Often it narrowed to one lane because some sections were under repair from rock slides and cave-ins. There were no pristine painted lines, no guardrails, and no enforced speed limits. When you added hairpin turns, heart-stopping drop-offs and chasms, plus traffic that included both large trucks and animal-drawn carts, the result was harrowing.

"If we make it safely back over the mountains, it will be a miracle," Jay said after a particularly close call with an oncoming truck. "I thought the river crossing was bad. It was nothing compared to this. My eyes hurt from squeezing them shut and I've had about ten heart attacks."

"It's all about your karma, Jay," Adam said with a grin, "whether you are ordained to pass into another life today or not. Stick close to Sidney. She will be okay, for her god Shiva is rescuing her from the jungle, remember?"

"Sidney's had a lot of close calls, Adam. Sticking close to her is not always such a good idea. If you only knew."

Jay was right. His words brought to mind all the narrow escapes in which I'd had to call on my true God to rescue me, and by that I didn't mean the guy wearing the Yankees baseball cap who was driving the car.

Just as Jay finished speaking, Shiva swerved into a turnout on the side of the road and pulled up to a concrete block building that apparently served as sort of a service station and general store. A crowd of men milled about the entrance, none of them looking at all friendly. I was suddenly acutely aware of being the only woman anywhere in sight.

Shiva, whose English was limited at best, graphically indicated the purpose of the stop.

"I'll just stay here with Sidney while you go, Jay," Adam said in a low voice. "When you return, I'll go."

Jay got out of the car and followed Shiva to the back of the building, which had apparently been dedicated to a certain function. The hostile gaze of the gathered men followed them as they walked and then the watchers turned back to us.

"Can you make it back to Kathmandu without visiting the facility, darling?" Adam asked, his eyes serious. "It's certain to be very basic and I think this might not be the best place for you to take a potty break."

I nodded, gazing at the silent, staring men.

Adam climbed out of the car, locked and closed the door, and stood defiantly in front of it, arms folded, returning the hostile stares.

In a moment Jay came back from around the building with Shiva. One of the men blocked his path and a short conversation ensued with Shiva translating and Jay emphatically shaking his head before returning to the car and exchanging places with Adam.

"What did he ask you, Jay?" I said.

"If you must know, he wanted to know if he could buy you, if you were for sale," Jay said, not kidding in the least. "I think we'd better get out of here the second Adam gets back to the car, don't you?"

20

IT WAS LATE BY THE time we finally rolled into the outskirts of Kathmandu. The sun was sinking behind the mountains, giving everything a pink and purple glow. I was happy to be back in the city and even happier to get safely back off the road to my clean hotel room and a warm bath. To say the elephant camp's facilities were Spartan would have been generous, and the harrowing ride through the mountains had certainly not been my favorite part of the journey.

Nor had the unsettling incident at the stop on the road. It is difficult for Western women to realize the chattel status that some women face daily in other parts of the world. There are educated, privileged women in India and Nepal who are powerful indeed, such as India's late Prime Minister, Indira Gandhi, or venerated, such as Mother Teresa. Scores more, however, particularly in remote areas, do not enjoy much status at all. The offer for me at the way station made me acutely aware that the freedom I enjoy in my everyday life is not shared by all my sisters.

I thanked Adam for his kindness in inviting us along in his car. Adam didn't come into the hotel with us. He stayed with the car, saying that he had a stop to make before dismissing Shiva. Jay also thanked him for the ride and hopped out to see to our bags.

"Adam," I said through the car window, "I really appreciate this. You were good to arrange it and invite us along. I know you didn't have to. You could easily have just taken off on your own, like Jasmine."

"Ah, but there was a selfish reason there, lass. I never thought of leaving you in the jungle. I wanted to bring you back with me so I could take you to the festival tonight in the heart of the old city. Are you still going with me?"

"Yes, of course. I'd love to. I'm looking forward to it. I'll tell Jay. What time?"

"Nine o'clock, after dinner. I'll meet you here at the front door. But not Jay, Sidney. You. Just you."

Oh. Wow. I looked full into those deep green eyes.

"I'll be here," I said, and climbed the steps to the hotel as the car rolled away.

My hotel room, as previously promised, was the same one I'd had before, as Brooke had requested. At least Sharma hadn't managed to farkel that up. And when I checked the safe I breathed a sigh of relief. The document Sharma had sold me was still there as I'd left it. I planned to show it to Jay and Brooke in the morning and get them to help me decide how to proceed. I relocked the safe, turned on the shower, and was soon luxuriating in the abundant hot water and scented soap.

Later, with squeaky-clean hair from that great shower and shampoo, I pulled on a silky black top and black pants and went in search of dinner and Brooke. In anticipation of the evening ahead I took special care with hair and makeup and added some new earrings and a spritz of perfume.

My outfit was chosen deliberately for the night at the festival. The blouse looked great, but it had long sleeves and the neckline was cut higher than it might have been for going out in the evening at home. The incident with the men on the road had made a profound impression on me. Even with Adam's protection, I did not want to wear something into the dark streets that might seem alluring to strangers.

At our agency we try to preach to our clients the importance of being mindful of the customs of a country when visiting. That doesn't mean that you have to act or dress exactly as the natives do. It does mean thinking about whether your thoughtless choices as a tourist may be considered just plain rude and even, among some groups, put your personal safety at risk.

I met Jay in the hall, and together we walked toward the main dining room where the evening meal was well underway.

"Well," he said, checking me out, "you sure cleaned up nice. You smell better too. What's the occasion? Got a hot date?"

"Yes," I said, "I do. With Adam." Then I told him all about it.

"And I can't go? Just you?"

"Yep. Just me."

He gave me a long, searching look. Sometimes Jay thinks he has a big say in my life.

"Well, okay, babe. I'll go on my own or with someone else, maybe Lucy and Justin. They just showed up. Guess they changed their minds about staying after the rest of us left."

We walked into the dining room and waited to be seated. I looked around for the others but didn't see anyone I knew.

"What about Brooke?" I asked as I took my seat and unfolded my napkin, "Have you seen her yet? I tried to call her room but there was no answer."

"No, but I spoke with Rahim. Brooke is feeling better and has gone to dinner with Jasmine and some of her movie friends. Then they are going on to the festival."

"Without Rahim? I thought he went everywhere with her."

"Remember, Jasmine has her own security, so Brooke gave Rahim the night off. He didn't seem pleased with that arrangement. He doesn't trust anyone else to look after her. I don't know where Mohit is. I haven't seen him and I forgot to ask Rahim. But I've got big news about Sharma. After we've ordered, I'll give you the scoop."

A waiter handed us a menu.

"Awwww," Jay said, "no rice and beans. What a disappointment! I was beginning to like having them for every meal."

"Just be glad you're here and not there, Jay. I am. I loved the elephant safari part but last night was too much. I barely slept at all. I thought something was crawling in my bed."

"Was it?"

"I'm not sure. I examined the cot with my flashlight but couldn't spot anything. It likely was just my imagination but even the thought made me itchy all over. The first thing I did when we got back here was to take an endless hot shower."

"Yeah, me too."

He closed his menu, and we told the waiter our selections.

"Well," Jay said, sipping from a glass of golden Chablis, "don't you want to hear the news?"

"Of course I do, especially as I can see you are dying to tell it."

"I am. I can hardly wait to email the office and let the boss know how well his pal Sharma turned out. Did I tell you he's long gone?"

I felt my jaw drop. "Who? Sharma? He's left us?"

"Yes. Jasmine told me all about it. He was gone when she got back to the hotel ahead of us. Sharma walked without paying the entire bill for this hotel, and no one knows for sure where he is now."

I stared at him, wide-eyed. "No kidding? Really?"

"Yes. Jasmine thinks he skipped across the border and is somewhere back in India. He booked us into that pitiful little dump in the jungle and pocketed the cash. I guess the dummy thought we wouldn't know the difference. The minute we left for the Terai, he blew. Brooke had to cover the tab for the hotel after she had already paid Sharma in advance for it. So she actually paid for the hotel accommodations twice, once to Sharma, then again to the hotel. He had not given the hotel a penny. He told them he would pay upon checkout, but then he disappeared. We were never booked into the real Tiger Tops either. Sharma just took the money for it and blew town, leaving Brooke holding the bag for everything. Brooke had paid him upfront for the whole tour."

"What a rat. I can't believe it!"

"Believe it. It's true. If it weren't for Brooke's cash, we'd be kicked out of this hotel and stranded. Luckily, Rahim has everyone's air tickets. Sharma disappeared without paying Rahim or Mohit for their services either, so Brooke covered that as well. Rahim said that she is furious but there's not a lot she can do about it just now."

"Where does that leave us?"

"Not sure. I'm emailing Silverstein that we need to talk as soon as possible. I thought we could speak with Brooke first to see what she's thinking."

"What a mess! But I'm not entirely surprised. There's little about Sharma that can be trusted. His price was apparently pretty low. I didn't trust that guy from the get-go."

"Me either. And if I could get my hands on him, I'd squash him like a bug."

Jay's eyes were glittering, and he looked as if he really meant what he said.

"Let me know if Sharma resurfaces, Jay. I need to talk to him."

"Really? Why on earth would you want to talk to him?"

"Because he sold me the real proof of Felix's murder, that's why, and I want to ask him a few more questions about it, like how he acquired it. I didn't tell you about it earlier because we were leaving for the jungle and there was no time to act on it, but now there is. I want to show it to you and Brooke in the morning and talk about how we can get it in the hands of the proper authorities. Even though Sharma's turned out to be a crook, I believe the document he sold me is genuine."

Then I told him all about it. He looked concerned and serious, not at all his usual jolly self.

"Have you told anyone else about this, Sidney?"

"No. Only you."

"Good. Please don't. We'll figure it out with Brooke, and only Brooke, tomorrow. I'm actually glad to find real proof of her suspicions, and I know Brooke will be too. I think she was worried that she might be losing her mind. This proves that her fears about her safety were real. But it also leaves us with a murderer, Sidney. Someone in our group gave Felix that poison. And thus someone must have poisoned the candy at the party too. We'll have to figure out who. Keep your mouth shut and be very careful. Don't you dare confide in anyone. No one can know you have that paper, not even Bonnie Prince Charlie. Understand?"

I nodded. We were so intent in our conversation that we were startled when a voice interrupted us.

"Well hello there, dears, may we join you? Am I interrupting something?"

I looked up to see Lucy standing beside Jay's chair, with Justin fast approaching behind her. They both looked fresh, and I guessed that the showers had been their first stop too. Lucy's makeup was perfect and every blonde hair was in place. Justin, as usual, wore clearly expensive slacks, an open-collared shirt, and a whiff of cologne. The scent of that cologne took me back to my unpleasant encounter with him at Khajuraho. I decided I really did not like Justin at all.

"Of course you may join us," I said. "We've just ordered." Jay and I moved our chairs to make room for them at the table. "Here, have a seat."

"*Merci*," Justin said, pulling out a chair for Lucy and signaling the waiter.

"Have you heard the news about Sharma?" Jay asked.

When they said no, Jay told them what he had just told

me, adding that he hated for Brooke to be out all that money, especially as a lot of it was spent for our benefit.

"Oh, I wouldn't worry a bit about that, Jay," Lucy said, sipping a ruby Cabernet. "Brooke has packs of money and if she's running a bit short she can borrow some from Jasmine."

"Is Jasmine rich, too?" I asked. "I know she's famous locally, if not internationally. I didn't know she is also wealthy." From Brooke, I knew that Jasmine had inherited a fortune from her Indian film director lover, but I wanted to see if Lucy had something else to share.

"Oh, my, yes, dear," Lucy said, nodding toward me. "She already was, you know, and now she'll be getting all of Felix's money."

"She will?" Jay asked. "Why is that?"

"Because she slept with him so he left it to her, that's why. I was in business with him, so I know," Justin answered in his unpleasant way, "That's what she does with men. That's where she gets all her fortune. She likes sleeping with different men. I think she even slept with Monsieur Sharma. *C'est une araignée*, a spider, that one. Luring victims into her web."

Ah, but you escaped her web, didn't you? I thought, laughing inwardly at the memory of him running down the hallway wearing only his underwear, dodging her shoes.

"Is she a good actress?" Jay asked.

"*Non*! She's not a good actress. She's a buffoon! Lucy can tell you about Felix and Jasmine. Lucy knew Felix better than anyone before Jasmine snared him. Lucy introduced him to Brooke and convinced her to hire him to manage her business. But Lucy didn't know all Jasmine's tricks in the bedroom, did you, *chérie*?"

There was an uncomfortable silence, the sort that happens whenever someone says something terribly awkward and rude. Lucy did not say a word, only fixed Justin with an icy glare.

"Moving right along," Jay said, "we were just discussing our plans for tonight. Sidney has a hot date, so if you two are going to the festival I might want to go with you if you'll have me."

"Why yes, of course you may," Lucy said, apparently recovering and once again her charming self. Her pleasant mask was back in place, her fury evident only in the measured politeness she used in speaking to Justin.

Glancing in his direction, she said, "We'd love to have Jay go with us, wouldn't we, Justin?" He gave a curt nod but did not second her words of welcome. He really was a most unpleasant man. *If I were Jay, and especially Lucy*, I thought, *I wouldn't want to go anywhere with him*. Lucy's relationship with the nasty little Frenchman was puzzling to me. I certainly wouldn't choose to be friends with him, neighbor or not.

"Who are you going with, dear?" Lucy asked, turning to me with her customary kind smile.

"Adam invited me," I said.

Lucy and Justin exchanged glances.

"Has he spoken to you of his wife, *chérie*?" Justin asked. "You are like her. She looked a lot like you."

"No, actually," I said, annoyed by his question. "He hasn't really discussed her much with me. Why should he?"

Justin gave one of his insolent shrugs, and threw Lucy another pointed glance.

"It was tragic," Lucy said. "Her name was Meghan and she was a lovely girl, full of life. Her death was so sudden, such a shame. It shocked us all. Justin is right, you know. You remind me of her too. She did look like you. She was tall, with long dark hair and lashes like yours."

Great, I thought. The man has asked me out because he thinks I'm a ghost. Just my luck.

Jay was tickled to hear what they had to say about Adam's dead wife, I could tell.

I knew I would hear a lot more from him later on the subject. Even as we were served an excellent meal, and the dinner conversation turned to other things, his eyes danced as he mouthed to me whenever the others weren't looking, "Marsh Curse, Marsh Curse, Marsh Curse."

21

AT THE HOTEL ENTRANCE, ADAM helped me into a motorized rickshaw and we were off, whizzing through the ancient streets toward an ancient festival in an ancient city. Everything about the core city of Kathmandu feels unbelievably old. I felt as if I were in a time machine, and only the warm grip of his strong arm around my waist as he helped me out of the rickshaw and guided me through the crowd reminded me that I was very much in the living present.

The festival was an explosion of light, color, smells and sound, bombarding the senses. The air was scented with the orange marigolds strung as necklaces for the statues of the gods, sandalwood incense, and the sizzling oil used to fry dumplings at street-side burners. We wandered, laughing, down the streets and alleys that meandered amid the many buildings, some made of wood and some of stone—two tall Westerners towering over the tiny beautiful people like Gulliver among the Lilliputians.

"Lady, look, lady, look!" and "my friend, my friend," peddlers shouted, trying to sell me bracelets, necklaces, scarves, and even, to my horror, bones set in silver.

Adam bought himself one of the sharp curved knives of the famed Gurkha regiment of the British Army, the fierce Nepali soldiers who were said to have so terrified the Argentine soldiers in the Falklands War. He bought me necklace after necklace, laughing his deep laugh and draping them over my head until I felt I must resemble one of the hundreds of statues of gods being worshipped with candles, flowers, and sticks of burning incense.

Young men ran in the streets, pulling the huge empty wooden carts used by the Living Goddess. The wheels of the enormous carts were also of wood, taller and thicker than a man, and it took teams of a dozen men or more to pull them. Once underway, the carts careened under their own weight through the crowded streets, and only the deep rumbling sound warned people to spring out of the way just in time to avoid being crushed to death under the giant wheels.

After a narrow escape of our own, Adam pulled me with him behind the safe shelter of a stone wall, and leaning down, kissed me, gently at first and then fiercely, pulling me close until I was breathless.

I closed my eyes and leaned into his strong, hard body, returning his embrace. His hands twisted in my long, wild hair as he pulled me tight against him.

"Oh, my dearest, my darling," he murmured, kissing my neck and pulling me even closer. His face was buried in my hair, and he hugged me so tightly I could hardly breathe. "My precious Meg …."

Meg?

I pulled free and stared at him for a moment in shock, searching his face. Then I whirled and took off, away from him, through the crowd.

"Sidney, wait!" he shouted. "I'm sorry, so sorry. I didn't mean …. It was a mistake. Come back! Forgive me …."

But the rest of his words were lost to me, swallowed up in the noises of the night, in the explosions of fireworks as I wove through the crowd.

I was shocked and embarrassed, and all I wanted to do at that moment was get away from him. I wanted to forget that the strong attraction I had felt between us and welcomed so freely was apparently intended for another woman, and a dead woman at that. How humiliating! I, Sidney Marsh, clearly meant nothing to this man except as a surrogate for his lost wife. I had been an idiot to imagine anything else. I wove swiftly through the crowd, ignoring his distant shouts as he attempted to follow me, tears streaming down my face, until I finally stopped to catch my breath and realized that he was no longer following. I had lost him, in more ways than one. As laughingly predicted by Jay, The Marsh Curse had struck me again, in full vengeance, and when I least expected it.

I marched on through the frenzied crowd, barely noticing the revelry swirling around me, trying to think and soothe my wounded pride. Finally calming down, I stopped acting like a jilted teenager and came to my senses, realizing that my own emotions and the shock of reality had caused me to totally overreact.

Now I had an even bigger problem. I had absolutely no idea where I was in the complicated network of medieval streets. I stopped and stepped out of the crowd into the shelter of an overhanging building to try to get my bearings. I did not speak the language, and the peddlers who might have understood me—the ones used to dealing with tourists—had packed up and gone. I was alone, lost and alone in the exuberant crowd.

I recalled earlier passing the plaza in front of the house of the Living Goddess, so I tried to retrace my steps. But I apparently took a wrong turn and now was really lost, even more so than I had been moments before.

The festival crowd thinned and then disappeared as I walked away from the center of the festival revelry, looking for a taxi. It wasn't long before I knew I was in real trouble. In my silly, heedless flight from Adam I had put myself in a grave situation. I had absolutely no idea where I was, or how to find my way back to the hotel. *Think, Sidney, think!* I told myself as I crept along the dark, now deserted streets, trying to discover the right direction. *Where is the way out? Where are the cabs? Was it this corner or that one? Did we turn here? Does that building look familiar?*

Finally, something did, and I turned into a street by a building that I seemed to remember passing earlier in the evening as we entered the old city. I stopped, finally catching my breath. After a moment I walked on, and it was then that I noticed a man walking behind me in the dark street with purpose, then another, on the opposite side. They were both grinning and watching me intently as they slipped from shadow to shadow.

Icy fingers of fear clutched my heart, and I walked faster, trying not to look back, but in a moment they were joined by two others. As their pace increased, narrowing the gap between them and me, stalking me like pack of wolves, so did mine. Soon I began to run, tears streaming down my face, and they followed, barely half a block behind me.

Just when I thought I would be caught, I dodged around a corner and an expensive car slid to a stop beside me. The window rolled down, and a silken arm beckoned, bracelets glinting in the car light. Only then did I realize that it was Jasmine.

I've never been so glad to see anyone before in my entire life. I looked back, and the men who had been stalking me were slinking back into the shadows, no longer in pursuit. All the negative thoughts I'd ever had about Jasmine evaporated in a wash of gratitude.

"Sidney," she shrieked, "what do you mean, walking these lonely streets by yourself in the night? Everyone is looking for you. When Brooke and I got to the hotel after dinner she wanted to speak with you but they said you had not returned. They are all back at the hotel. Brooke was very worried and I had this car so she sent me to look for you. Get in, get in quickly."

Her security guard held the door for me, and I climbed in, sinking into the deep leather seats in profound relief. What a close call I'd had! And what a fool I'd been, unfortunately not for the first time.

There was simply no rational explanation I could give Jasmine for my chaotic evening, and she didn't want to hear it anyway after I was stupid enough to tell her that I'd gone to the festival with Adam. At the mention of his name, anger flared in her eyes. Too late I remembered that he had rejected her advances and that she had been not at all pleased about it.

The car rolled smoothly away. The security man was in the front seat with the driver, and her assistant sat in the back with me and Jasmine.

"So you are with this dog, Adam, and now you come to me for help, is that it, Sidney?" she hissed, eyes flashing.

Terrified that the temperamental actress would stop the car and put me out again to brave the night alone, I attempted to mollify her anger. I told her that Adam and I were only friends, that I had been separated from him in the crowd, then got lost and couldn't find my way back from the festival. No way was I mentioning what had happened between us when the mere fact of my presence with him that evening caused her jealousy to flare.

My nonchalant manner as I downplayed my date with Adam seemed to mollify her somewhat and she fell silent, turning her back to me, watching the dark streets as we rushed through the night.

I relaxed and closed my eyes, resting my aching head on the back of the seat, my mind flooded with the extremes of the last few hours. I was thankfully headed back to Jay and the safety of the hotel, and the morning flight would take me back to Delhi and then home, to my dear little apartment in New York, where life would be calm again.

I would give Sharma's paper to Brooke, I thought, let her handle it as she saw fit, turn in my detective badge and go home. Simple as that. *Calf-rope*, my Uncle Earl would say. *Stick a fork in me, I'm done.*

"Sidney," Jasmine said, her voice silky and musical once more, "Brooke tells me you think my dear Felix did not die a normal death after all, that Mr. Sharma bribed the official to change the report and now has given you the true one. Is this so? Do you have a document proving his death from the fruit of the suicide tree?"

I was shocked by her question. How could she know about the paper? Brooke didn't know about it. I hadn't told her yet, or anyone else. Only Jay and Sharma knew. Even in my foolish moments of intimacy I had not confided in Adam. And I knew Jay would not have told her or anyone.

I opened my eyes and looked at her. She was smiling the wide smile that had dazzled hundreds of her adoring fans.

And in that moment, I knew. I remembered Mohit's singsong words as he spoke of the potent poison of the suicide tree, "A lovely fragrant tree with white flowers and dark green leaves, but its seeds bring death. It flourishes in the Kerala region." Kerala. Jasmine's home town.

"Yes, Jasmine," I said, thinking fast. "I believe that he was deliberately killed, but what proof could I, an American tourist, have of such a thing? That is ridiculous. I am not the police."

"No, but you could cause inquiries to be made, and those inquiries could bring results. This is not your world, Sidney. In this world there are many eyes, many ears. It is known to me that foolish Sharma gave the report to you. He told me so himself before he died."

"Sharma is dead?"

"Yes," she said, again with the radiant smile, "The night after we left for the Terai, Sharma fell beneath the wheels of a festival cart and was crushed. Such accidents are not uncommon at such times in such a crowd. Just another tragic accident, no? I know you have the paper, Sidney. Sharma told me himself. Now you must give it to me. Where is it? Must I have you stripped to find it?"

"In my room," I said. "Hidden in my room at the hotel. Take me back there and I will give it to you." I suddenly knew why my bag had temporarily gone missing at Big Tiger Watch Camp. Jasmine had known even then about the document and thought I might have it with me.

She laughed then, a raucous laugh, enjoying my terror.

"Oh no, Sidney. I cannot afford to do that. I can search your room and destroy this paper without you. Unfortunately you will not be there to hand it over yourself. You will only be a sad reminder of what can happen to a foreign girl wandering alone in a strange country at night. Remember the sad newspaper stories of the girl on the bus in Delhi? You will die like her."

She tapped the driver on the shoulder. The car pulled to the side and stopped.

At Jasmine's nod, the man on my left opened his door and pulled me out, forcing my arms behind me as he dragged me to the side of the road. The other man got out of the front seat to help, dodging my kicks and stuffing a filthy rag in my mouth to stifle my screams. Neither said a word. The second man opened the car trunk and removed a length of long thin rope.

"Tie her to that post and leave her," Jasmine hissed. "The jackals of the streets will soon find her. Before she dies she will know what it means to cross Jasmine."

The two burly men tied me tightly to the post. My struggles were nothing to them. Minutes later they were back in the car. Then the car doors slammed and they drove Jasmine swiftly away. I heard her mocking laughter through the open windows grow ever fainter as the car's taillights disappeared around a corner.

22

I DIDN'T DIE, BECAUSE THE jackals didn't find me.

Jay and Adam did, accompanied by Brooke, Rahim, and a whole posse of police.

Poor, guilt-stricken Adam had launched an all-out search for me when he got back to the hotel and found that I had not returned. Jay, knowing all the stupid stunts I have somehow managed to pull in my life, pushed the panic button as well, and it's a good thing they did or I might not be here to tell the tale. Even our journalist friends from the bar joined in the search. It was all pretty embarrassing later, but at the time I could only feel gratitude.

A watch was put on my room and the hotel security caught Jasmine and her assistants breaking in to steal Sharma's document. Jasmine denied it all, and as she was led away, demanded that her lawyer be called, insisting she could explain everything.

We all agreed that Jasmine would have a lot of explaining to do, particularly as seeds of the suicide tree were found by the police, hidden in the makeup bag in her room.

Her assistants, who blamed each other under separate

questioning for pushing Sharma under the wheels of the cart at the festival, were taken away with her.

Before she left for the airport, Brooke pulled me aside to say how sorry she was for putting me in harm's way, and to thank me for exposing Jasmine as the murderess.

"I'm not quite sure how you do it, Sidney, and I'm not sure you do either, but you always manage to ferret out the truth and end up on top, don't you? You really might want to be a bit more careful in the future, though. You've had more than a few narrow escapes, haven't you, my dear?"

"Too many, Brooke. I hate to admit it, but I think Jay may be right. I need to dial it down somehow in the future before I get myself in one scrape too many. I'm just going to go back to work in New York and try to mind my own business. If I still have a job, that is, after all this."

"I wouldn't worry a lot about that, Sidney. I spoke with your Mr. Silverstein myself this morning on that very subject. I called him because I wanted to be sure he fully realizes what a valuable employee he has in you."

"You did? I appreciate that more than you know, Brooke. I love my job, and I don't want to lose it. Thank you for that, and thank you for making this lovely trip possible for us, too. Except for the last few hours, I had a wonderful time. This has been an amazing trip."

"I'm glad you feel that way, my dear. I had a good time, too, in spite of everything. But now, I am so relieved that it's over. Fearing that someone wishes you deadly harm is not a good way to live. Perhaps I'll see you on another trip sometime soon. I understand that the new owner of your agency is planning quite an expansion."

"New owner of my agency? The agency's been sold?"

"Yes, indeed. Mr. Silverstein said he would tell you all about it when you get back to New York. Goodbye for now, Sidney. Have a safe journey home, and give my best regards to Jay. I'm leaving in a few moments and don't expect to see him again before my car arrives."

As Brooke finished speaking, Rahim and Mohit appeared to escort her to the front entrance where her car, Lucy, and Justin were waiting. I waved goodbye to them as the car rolled smoothly away. Brooke, Lucy, and Justin were headed to the airport, then bound ultimately for Lucy's home in St. Tropez to rest and recover.

I refused Adam's invitation to do the same in Scotland. He made it clear that the invitation was open-ended and was there for me if I changed my mind in the future. Like my Southern sister Scarlett, I decided that I would think about that tomorrow.

Mohit had stood beside me silently, with palms folded, bowing toward Brooke's retreating car in a traditional Hindu farewell until it was no longer in sight.

Then he turned to me, placed his palms together, and bowed again before saying, "Goodbye, lady." With one of his intent stares through his thick, round glasses, he added, "It may be that we will meet again. Who can know what will come? It is written that our fortunes await us because of our deeds. Take great care in the future, my lady, for you are pursued by your karma."

After all was said and done, after signing a statement for the police and leaving my contact information, I was just happy to be climbing aboard a plane at Tribhuvan International Airport and heading back home with Jay.

After stowing his red turban in the overhead, he asked, "Do you think we really still have a job, especially now that we seem to have a new owner?" He settled in his seat and fastened his seatbelt. "He hasn't responded to my email and my call went to voicemail."

The big plane pushed back from the gate and taxied toward the runway.

"Who knows?" I said. "We should. I didn't really do anything this time that people could blame on me, did I?"

"You never do, babe," he said, shaking his head. "You never

do. You may get blamed for this or you may not. I don't know. With you, somehow these things just happen. I think Mohit might be right. It may be your karma."

I was quiet for a moment, considering just what my karma might include.

"Jay," I said, as the big plane lifted off the tarmac and headed west, bound for New York, "It's not really finished. The mystery, I mean. We never really discovered exactly who tried to poison Brooke, did we? That's what we were really hired to do. We only proved that Jasmine poisoned Felix."

"Yes, we did. Lucy, Brooke, and I figured out what happened with the chocolate while you were frolicking at the festival with Adam. In all that happened afterwards I forgot to tell you. Turns out, no one tried to poison Brooke after all, Sidney. The intended victim was always Felix."

"What? What do you mean? Was the poisoned candy all just Brooke's imagination?"

"No. It was real, all right, and she's lucky it didn't kill her. I'll bet my turban it turns out to be the same toxic Indian poison that did it for Felix. But it was not ever intended for Brooke, only Felix. Lucy remembered that Felix was sitting next to Brooke that night, and in her haste Jasmine must have switched out the good candy box for the poisoned one at the wrong place. Jasmine didn't want to kill Brooke, she wanted to kill Felix. She just made a mistake with the candy."

"That was a pretty big mistake."

"Yes. She made other mistakes as well, but Brooke didn't notice them. Lucy has sharp eyes, though. Lucy remembers seeing Jasmine coming back to the table with a candy box in her gloved hand when she returned from the restroom. We think she injected the candy with the poison there before placing it back at what she thought was Felix's place. Lucy particularly noticed Jasmine's long gloves that evening. She thought them an odd touch at the time but put it down to Jasmine's dramatic way of dressing. Brooke was never the intended victim. It was always Felix."

"She killed him for his money. She really was a spider, like Justin said, wasn't she?"

"Yep. Felix had made Jasmine his heir and they were not getting along, so he had to die before he could change his will. When the candy attempt failed she pretended to make up with him until she could try again. Brooke's moving house party in India was the perfect opportunity."

"Jay, why didn't Lucy tell Brooke all this before? Felix might still be alive."

"Because Lucy didn't know Brooke's candy was poisoned. Brooke kept it a deep secret, remember? She even thought that Lucy might have poisoned the candy."

"If Brooke had told," I whispered, almost to myself, thinking back on all that had happened, "Felix might be alive, and we might have never gone to India or Nepal. We never know, do we, what our simplest actions might set in motion."

Jay reclined his seat and stretched out, making his nest for the long journey home. "Like Mohit said, babe," he murmured, with a twinkle of amusement in his warm brown eyes, "'Your karma pursues you.' That's all it is. Jasmine might have easily gotten away with it all and moved on to her next victim if it hadn't been for Sidney, Girl Detective. I think you, Sidney, of all the people I have ever known, must be totally pursued by your karma, don't you?"

Photograph by Chad Mellon

MARIE MOORE IS A NATIVE Mississippian. She graduated from Ole Miss, married a lawyer in her hometown, taught junior high science, raised a family, and worked for a small weekly newspaper—first as a writer and later as Managing Editor. She wrote hard news, features, and a weekly column, sold ads, did interviews, took photos, and won a couple of MS Press Association awards for her stories.

In 1985, Marie left the newspaper to open a retail travel agency, and for the next fifteen years, she managed the agency, sold travel, escorted group tours, sailed on nineteen cruises, and visited over sixty countries. The Sidney Marsh Murder Mystery Series was inspired by those experiences.

Marie also did location scouting and worked as the local contact for several feature films, including *Heart of Dixie, The*

Gun in Betty Lou's Handbag, and Robert Altman's *Cookie's Fortune*.

In mid-1999, because of her husband's work, Marie sold her travel agency and moved to Jackson, MS, then New York City, Anna Maria Island, FL, and Arlington, VA. She and her husband now live in Memphis, TN, and Holly Springs, MS.

Marie is an active member of Mystery Writers of America and Sisters in Crime.

Side Trip to Kathmandu is the third book in the Sidney Marsh Murder Mystery series, which began with *Shore Excursion*. For more information, go to www.mariemooremysteries.com.

Made in the USA
Lexington, KY
07 March 2015